BRANDED FOR YOU

Formatting and Interior Design by Bella Media Management.

First Pink Zebra Publishing Paperback Edition

13 Digit ISBN: 978-1480297180

BRANDED FOR YOU

Cheyenne McCray

Pink zebra publishing
Scottsdale, Arizona

CHAPTER 1

"I think you should just kill the bastard and be done with it."
Tess ran her fingers through her chin-length wavy blonde hair and
opened up a small notebook she always carried in her purse. She
set the notebook on the kitchen table and drew a hangman with
X's for eyes and its tongue lolling out to the side of its downturned
mouth. She wrote BART in block letters beneath the stick figure.

Megan Wilder braced her elbow on the table as she looked
at the drawing, her chin in her palm as she looked at her sister's
simplistic drawing. "You think?"

Tess gave an emphatic nod, fire sparking in her cobalt blue
eyes. "I'll help you hide the body."

"That would solve a lot of problems." Megan raised her head and leaned back in her chair. "What about that woman?"

"They both deserve the same fate." Tess drew a hangwoman with long straw-like hair, the figure hanging from a post by a noose. Beneath the figure she wrote BITCH in block letters. "We'll bury the skinny witch in the same grave."

"Works for me." Megan wanted to laugh even though she usually had a hard time smiling about some things, like her ex-husband, Bart. "But for now we need to get back to packing so that we can get out of this place. I've had enough of it here."

"You're no fun." Tess gave Megan an evil grin as she closed the notebook and tucked it back into her purse. "I think we should plot the jerk's demise first, then finish loading all of your stuff into the moving van."

"De-mize?" A little girl's voice came from behind Tess's chair. "What's de-mize?"

Megan leaned sideways to get a peek at Jenny, Tess's five-year-old daughter, as she rounded the chair where her mother sat. The girl had slashed red lipstick around and across her lips and held a naked baby doll with a blonde frizzy ponytail and one eye glued shut. The doll had red lipstick across her face, too.

"Where are Bette's clothes?" Megan asked her niece as she tried not to laugh.

"I packed them." Jenny came closer and stood between Tess and Megan as she pointed toward the bedroom. "In your little pink suitcase with all of your makeup."

"Ah." Megan wasn't sure she managed to keep a look of amusement off of her face. "I see you found my lipstick. You look pretty."

"Thank you, Aunt Megan." Jenny looked at her mother who

didn't look as amused. "What's de-mize?"

"It means that if we don't get all of this stuff packed up, we're going to be late." Tess pushed her chair away from the table. "You need to stay out of Aunt Megan's makeup. Let's put Bette's clothes in your suitcase so that Aunt Megan has room for the rest of her toiletries."

"Okay." Jenny took her mother's hand. "I put Bette's magic bottle in with the makeup too."

"Let's make sure you put it in your baby bag," Tess said, as they walked away.

For a moment a sense of sadness went through Megan as she watched her niece take her mother's hand. Megan had wanted children so badly but Bart had put it off and then had destroyed their marriage. Now she was in her thirties with no relationship and no children in sight.

Tess and Jenny entered Megan's bedroom. Which had been Bart's bedroom, too.

A sick feeling clenched Megan's belly and tears pricked the back of her eyes. It was the way he'd left her that had cut so deeply, the way he'd told her he was leaving her for another woman.

Barb's not fat like you.

The words kept ringing in Megan's ears.

Barb's not fat like you.

Megan gritted her teeth and got up from her chair then shoved it up against the table. She forced tears away before they could leak from her eyes. It had been just over two months since the divorce was final, seven months since he'd left her for the other woman. But sometimes the pain still felt fresh. She knew she was better off without Bart, but that didn't mean it hurt any less.

A lifetime of not being thin enough to be popular in school, of not being slender like everyone else in her family, and being blindsided the one person who should have had her back—her ex. It was no wonder that the scars never seemed to heal. She'd think she was fine and then *bam*, she'd get sideswiped once again.

"*I'm thirty-two years old,*" Megan had said to her counselor after Bart left her, when the woman wanted to talk about Megan's past. "*I should be over what was said to me while I was growing up by my parents and the kids I went to school with.*"

"*Don't minimize what you went through,*" the counselor had said. "*Those kinds of scars run deep and you need to face them and recognize them for what they are.*"

Megan had stopped going to counseling when she'd decided to follow her parents and sister to Arizona. There was nothing left for her here in New Mexico. She wondered if she should find a counselor once she got to Prescott, but then thought it was more fun plotting Bart's death with Tess. A counselor might not find that amusing.

Sometimes Megan wondered if she was making the right choice. Her parents weren't easy people to be around and she'd never lived up to their expectations, despite the fact that she'd been successful in her career as a graphic designer. It wasn't good enough for them.

She relaxed her jaws and her fingers. She wasn't going to continue to second-guess herself.

A new chapter started in her life now, at this very moment, and she intended her book to end up with a happy ending. She was worth it. She deserved it.

She took a deep breath and closed her eyes then slowly exhaled. When she opened her eyes again she shook off all of the negativity and started toward the kitchen.

In the divorce settlement, she'd kept the house in Albuquerque and Bart had taken the cabin in the mountains. First chance she'd had after the divorce, she put the home up for sale and a buyer snatched it up almost right away. It was a cash transaction, so they hadn't had to deal with a lender. The sale went through smoothly. Now she just needed to get out of the house so that the new owners could move in.

She grabbed a small cardboard box and metal clinked against metal as she packed up the silverware drawer. Once it was full, she marked the box *kitchen* using a Sharpie, then taped the box shut with clear plastic packing tape. When that was finished, she packed another box with the pots and pans that she'd left out to use until moving day.

"Are you all right?" Tess walked up and set a stack of fluffy bathroom towels on the kitchen table. "You look like you're pretty deep in thought."

Megan gave her sister the brightest smile she could muster. "Just coming up with new ways to dispose of what's-his-name."

"Good." Tess blew loose strands of hair out of her face. She couldn't help but look adorable with her petite frame, slender body, and heart-shaped face. Her blonde hair was fluffed around her face, and she appeared younger than her thirty-seven years. "Once we get a plan down, we'll do away with the bastard."

Megan laughed. She adored her older sister who'd always been there for her from the time they were young. There was a five-year age difference, but Tess had always watched out for Megan. Tess had been her defender when they were young and her staunch supporter. Megan had been equally protective over Tess. That didn't mean they hadn't fought or argued as kids. At times Tess would get impatient with her younger sister who followed her around as much as possible. But all in all, they'd always been good friends.

Tess pushed her fingers through her hair. "Once we get you settled in Prescott, we need to find you a man. You have so much going for you."

"Like what?" Megan shook her head. "I need to shed a few pounds first."

"You look terrific." Tess put her hands on her hips. "You're just down because of that ass you married. Don't let him have that kind of power over you. You're curvy and sexy and you just need to feel good about yourself."

Megan smiled at her sister. "You always know how to make me feel better." Megan wasn't given to pity parties, but at this moment it was hard because memories of the last few years kept slapping her in the face every time she looked around the house she'd called home. She was truly glad she was no longer with her ex but that didn't mean the memories of what he'd put her through didn't still hurt.

"Older sisters know best," Tess grinned. "While we're at it, once we get to Arizona, we need to go shopping and get you some cute clothes, like jeans that will show off your beautiful ass-ets."

Megan laughed. "So now my ass is beautiful."

"You betcha." Tess nodded.

"Speaking of finding a man." Megan taped the box shut as she spoke. "You should follow your own advice. Maybe you should find yourself a hot cowboy."

"There are plenty of those in Arizona." Tess smiled. "A lot of nice eye-candy."

Tess might be noticing the sexy cowboys, but Megan was sure she wasn't letting anyone pursue her. Ever since her husband, Steve, had died in a car accident, Tess had remained closed off when it came to men. She'd loved Steve with a passion that mad Megan envious. After her husband's death Tess had followed their parents from Albuquerque to Prescott to help with the family restaurant.

"I need more than just eye candy." Megan leaned against the counter. "Bart was as good looking as any man. That didn't get me far. I would settle for eye broccoli. These days I need a little more substance."

Tess laughed. "Just keep a positive attitude. There's a meal-in-one out there for you, which would include dessert. Just stay positive."

Megan looked around the kitchen and at the living room. "Everything is close to being finished."

Tess gestured toward Megan's room. "Jenny's busy with her dolls on the carpet in your room, and I've put the makeup out of reach. So for now, the little monster is busy and not underfoot. I'm going to start taking what little is left in the house out to the moving van."

Megan went to her sister. "Thank you. For everything."

"That's what sisters are for." Tess took Megan's hands. "You were there for me every step of the way when Steve died. I want to be here for you just as much."

"You have been." Megan hugged Tess and caught her soft honeysuckle scent. "You're the best sister a girl could want."

"Ditto." Tess kissed Megan on the cheek. "Now, let's get a

move-on," she said before she headed outside with the silverware box.

Megan bounced back to her old self, pushing aside painful and negative thoughts to enjoy her sister and her niece as they helped her get ready for her move to Arizona. It was a new day filled with exciting possibilities.

"Why Mom and Dad picked such a small area in Northern Arizona, I'll never understand," Tess said as she came back in the house for another box. "I'd hoped they'd move somewhere like the southern part of the state. Maybe Tucson, as opposed to the Prescott area."

"I liked the place when I visited," Megan said. "With a hundred thousand people in the area, Prescott is not really small."

"It's okay." Tess shrugged. "I would just like something even bigger. Tucson has about a million people, close to the same population as Albuquerque."

"But you don't want anything as big as the Phoenix metro area," Megan said.

"No, four million people is too much for me." For padding, Tess scrunched the bathroom towels around the dishes Megan had just packed.

Megan grabbed the box tape. "Maybe you just need to get used to Prescott."

Tess folded the flaps on the dishware box and held them closed while Megan sealed it. "Yeah, you're probably right."

"Do you miss New Mexico?" Megan asked her sister.

"Not really," Tess said. "Like you, there's nothing left here for me but memories too hard to bear."

Megan rested her hand on Tess's shoulder a moment before

she picked up the dishware box and took it out to the big yellow rental truck that she'd be driving soon. It was still early morning and they were close to hitting the road. Last night they'd carried out most of the boxes with friends helping to load what little furniture Megan was keeping. Tess and her daughter had caught a flight to Albuquerque a few days ago in order to make the road trip to Arizona with Megan. Tess would be driving Megan's red Toyota Camry.

Megan slid the dishware box inside the truck then headed back into the house where she grabbed another box. It only took a few more trips by both Tess and Megan before the truck was loaded. The last things they loaded were the kitchen table and chairs. With the leaf out, the table wasn't too heavy.

Just as Megan started to follow her sister back into the house, a gold car she didn't recognize pulled into the driveway and the driver parked. Megan frowned and narrowed her gaze then felt a rush of pain and anger as her ex-husband got out of the car.

"Hi, Megan," Bart said as he shut the car door behind him. He walked toward her, his expression pleasant as if he was just a good friend. His cologne, as usual, was nearly overpowering. He glanced at the moving van. "You're moving? Did you sell the house?"

Megan straightened and raised her chin. Like hell she was going to engage in a conversation with him. "What do you want?"

"Where are you moving to?" he asked.

It was none of his business and she wasn't about to tell him anything personal. She gritted her teeth before asking, "Why are you here?"

"I keep forgetting to pick up my golf clubs," he said as he looked toward the front door. "I came by to get them."

"You're too late." Megan tried to remain calm. His presence made her feel anything but. "I donated all of the crap you left to the Salvation Army."

"You what?" Bart's features turned from pleasant to angry. "Those were mine."

Megan shrugged and had the desire to laugh. "I told you at least ten times in the last seven months to get your stuff. You never bothered to come by. What was I supposed to do, deliver them to you?"

"You b—" he started.

"Get out of here, Bart." Tess's voice came from behind Megan, cutting off Bart's sentence. "Megan doesn't want anything to do with you."

Bart ignored Tess. "You owe me for those clubs," he snarled at Megan.

"You should have taken them with you when you left with that woman." Megan hoped her features looked calm and didn't show the churning anger inside her. "You didn't, so, your loss."

"Go buy yourself some new ones." Tess came to stand beside Megan, arms folded across her chest. "And stop bothering Megan."

"Get out of here." Megan had to fight not to clench her hands into fists.

Bart looked like he was going to tear into her verbally like he used to. Instead, he turned and strode back to the car. He jerked the door open, climbed in and started the vehicle, then backed up the vehicle. The tires spun in the gravel as his car shot out of the driveway.

"I sure didn't need that." Megan sighed. The last thing she'd wanted imprinted in her mind before leaving New Mexico was her ex-husband's snide features.

"Ignore him." Tess took Megan by the arm. "Fart's a loser. Come on in and we'll give the place a once over."

Tess drew Megan back into what had been her home and now was nothing but a shell. "It cracks me up every time you call him that," Megan said

"Well he isn't deserving of respect," Tess said. "And besides, with all that awful cologne, the guy stinks, so it fits."

Megan laughed. "Thanks Tess, I needed that. I need to just get him out of my mind."

When they were finished making sure that everything was out of the house, Megan stood for a moment in the doorway as Tess and Jenny waited outside for her. Megan looked over the living room that now only had the cable from the satellite TV sticking out of the wall. The shutters were closed tight, no sunshine leaking in. The place looked stark and naked and felt as hollow as her heart.

Megan thought about the five years she'd spent in this house. She had wondered if she'd miss the place but as she looked over the empty living room and kitchen, she knew she wouldn't.

She smiled to herself. Everything would be fine. Life was good and she had a new life just waiting for her to grab onto and hold on for the ride.

CHAPTER 2

Megan shaded her eyes with her hand and looked up at the Ferris wheel as it turned against the clear late September sky. A breeze brushed her cheeks as she watched the small figures in the colorful seats and she shivered, more from a memory than from the cool air.

Thoughts of the last time she had been on a Ferris wheel went through her mind. Her cousin had scared her to death by rocking the seat when they were stopped at the very top and she'd been so sure they were going to fall to their deaths. She hadn't been on a Ferris wheel since.

She turned her attention toward the ticket booths where a steady flow of people entered the fairgrounds. Her sister and niece should be here at any time. Tess didn't normally run so late.

It was a Thursday and Tess had planned to take the afternoon off from the restaurant. What was keeping her?

Megan wiped her palms on her jeans, brushing dust from them as her gaze drifted over the crowd at the Yavapai County Fair. People walked to and from the exhibit halls housing vegetables, jams, canned foods, arts and crafts, and any other number of homemade or homegrown items. The prizewinners were draped with blue, red, and white ribbons indicating the prize won, and the best of each class were pinned with champion purple rosettes.

Other people headed to the carnival side of the county fair from which a cacophony of sounds emanated. Smells of corndogs, cotton candy, fry bread, and popcorn drifted over from the carnival and she pressed a hand to her belly, which rumbled from hunger. She really needed to watch what she ate, but the carnival food smelled so good. Her hips would never forgive her but she wanted a churro in the worst way.

While she waited for Tess and Jenny, Megan wandered toward the livestock building to watch the 4-H kids handle sheep, calves, and hogs they'd raised for show. Many of the animals would be auctioned off sometime this weekend with the champions taking home the highest dollar amounts.

As she reached the livestock buildings she saw that the place was alive with 4-H'ers feeding and watering their animals and preparing them for show. People wandered up and down the straw strewn dirt aisles, admiring the livestock.

Megan walked up to an arena fence and put her hands on the top rung as she watched a group of 4-H'ers showing Suffolk sheep. The black-faced and black legged lambs' white wool was shaved down almost to the skin.

A burning sensation caused a prickle at her nape. She felt like she was being watched. She glanced over her shoulder and a flutter traveled through her midsection when she saw that a cowboy was directly behind her...and he was looking right at her.

He was tall and muscular and his back was up against a cottonwood tree, thumbs hooked in the pockets of his dark blue Wrangler jeans that molded muscular thighs. He wore a light blue shirt with the sleeves rolled up to his elbows and the hair on his forearms was golden against his tan skin. He pushed up the brim of his western hat with one finger as he looked at her.

The tips of her ears burned as she glanced away, turning her attention back to the 4-H kids in the arena. The dangerously sexy cowboy couldn't have been showing interest in her. Men as sexy as this one seemed to prefer women with cute, petite figures rather than ladies with full curves.

She tried to pay attention to the 4-H'ers but she still had the feeling that he was watching her. It was all she could do not to look over her shoulder again.

"Know any of the kids out there?" a deep voice said just behind her.

Startled, she glanced at the man who had spoken and saw that it was the sexy cowboy who had been watching her. She met his blue eyes that were the color of faded denim as his lips curved into a slow, sensual smile. Heat flushed through her from her head to her toes.

It took her a moment to compose herself. She shook her head. "I don't know anyone here. I'm waiting for my sister and my niece."

He moved beside her and looked at the girls and boys who were showing the lambs. He rested one arm on the top rung of the fence as he gestured to a boy on the end. "That's my nephew, Brian."

It gave her an excuse to look away from the cowboy so she studied the boy. "He's a cute kid."

"He is." The man spoke in a low drawl and she glanced back to him. "I'm Ryan McBride," he said and held out his hand.

"I'm Megan." She offered him a smile as she took his hand. "Megan Wilder."

The warmth of his touch traveled straight through her. His grip was firm, his hand callused from hard work.

"When is your sister getting here?" he asked as he released Megan's hand.

"Tess was supposed to be here already." Megan dug in her pocket and grasped her cell phone. "I think I'd better call her." When she pulled her phone out of her pocket she saw that she'd missed a call. "Looks like my sister called and left a message."

Megan brought the phone to her ear and listened to the voice-mail.

"Hi, Megan." Tess sounded a little harried as she left the message. "Jenny has a fever so I need to keep her home. Sorry we have to miss out on spending time with you at the fair." Tess ended the message with, "Call me tonight."

Megan lowered the phone and met Ryan's gaze. "My niece has a fever so they're not going to make it to the fair. Looks like I'm on my own."

"I've got a better idea," he said with a smile. "Why don't you spend the afternoon with me?"

Her eyes widened a little in surprise. "I don't know you."

His lips curved with amusement. "No better way to get to

know me."

"I can't argue with that." She glanced toward the ring where the 4-H'ers were being presented with blue, red, and white ribbons. Brian was accepting a large purple ribbon with a rosette. "Looks like your nephew just won the grand champion prize for his lamb."

The crowd around the arena clapped. Ryan and Megan joined in.

"Is that why you're here?" she asked Ryan as the 4-H'ers walked their lambs out of the ring. "To see your nephew?"

"In part," Ryan said. "I'm also a 4-H leader. I help a group of local kids raise cattle."

"That's great." She smiled. "It must be rewarding."

He gave a nod. "It is."

"Do you have any more kids in your 4-H club showing livestock now?" she asked.

"My 4-H'ers finished up this morning." He gestured to the livestock building. "Have you had a chance to walk through?"

"Not yet." She shook her head.

"You're new in this area." He rested one arm on the top rail of the arena fence as he studied her. "How about letting me show you around?"

She tilted her head to the side. "How do you know I'm new?"

He gave her a teasing grin. "I have a sense about these things."

"Are you sure about that?" she asked.

"No doubt in my mind." His blue eyes held hers. "So how about it?"

The way he looked at her made heat travel straight through her belly. She swallowed. "All right."

He gave a sexy little smile. "We can start in the livestock

building."

She slipped her hands in her back pockets as they walked side-by-side under the rooftop that covered the livestock. It was open on all sides, the shade cooling the air even more. They headed down dirt aisles that were well kept. Smells of livestock, manure, dirt, and hay were heavy on the air.

As they strolled down the aisles, adults, teenagers, and younger children greeted Ryan. He stopped to talk with the kids, admiring their bulls, dairy cows, and calves, and congratulating the prizewinners. She gathered that he'd taught a lot of the 4-H'ers about raising and showing their animals.

"These kids will take their livestock to the state fair at the end of October," he said as they moved on to the sheep and dairy goats. "Our 4-H'ers represent us well."

As they walked, she enjoyed talking with Ryan and listening to stories he recounted about some of the kids he'd worked with over the years. He was easy to talk with and he made her feel comfortable, as if she'd known him for a while rather than just having met him. From the number of people who greeted him, it was clear he was well known and well liked.

After they'd made their way through the livestock buildings, including the building that housed chickens, ducks, and geese, they went through the exhibit halls. In the exhibit halls it was a little quieter and not as many people stopped Ryan to talk.

"Did you move here or are you just visiting?" Ryan asked as they looked at a quilt exhibit.

"I moved to Prescott a month ago to be closer to my family." She pushed a lock of shoulder-length brown hair behind her ear. "For the time being I'm staying with them but I plan to buy my own house as soon as things settle down."

Before he could ask her more questions about her family, she hurried to ask him questions. "Where do you live?"

"I have a ranch just outside of Prescott Valley," he said. "I raise cattle and horses, and have a small flock of Suffolk sheep."

"Are you related to Officer John McBride?" she asked.

Ryan nodded. "John is my cousin."

"He almost ticketed me for speeding." She gave Ryan a rueful smile. "I wasn't paying attention to my speed on the highway the day I moved here. He was nice enough to let me off with a warning."

Ryan laughed. "So you're a little speed demon?"

"I have a lead foot at times." She shook her head. "I really need to watch my speed better."

"Where are you from?" he asked.

"Albuquerque." She glanced at a photography exhibit and stopped as she spotted a picture of a cowboy riding a bull. The shot was so clear, so vivid, that she half expected the image of the cowboy and bull to move. "I don't know a lot about photography, but that's a terrific shot."

"That's my youngest brother, Creed. He's a world champion bull rider." Ryan came up beside her. "He's newly married to a gal who's from the San Rafael Valley in the southern part of the state."

"How cool, to have a world-famous bull rider in the family." She noticed the purple rosette next to the photograph. "I must have good taste. It's the exhibit winner."

"What did you do in New Mexico?" Ryan asked as they continued walking.

She shoved her hands in her front pockets. "I'm a graphic designer."

"What are you going to do in Prescott?" he asked.

She glanced up at him. "I'm going to continue what I was doing. I can work from home since my business is Internet based."

Ryan and Megan walked outside of the cool exhibit hall and into the bright sunshine. They were closer now to the carnival side of the fairgrounds and the music was much louder. The yellow grass was worn down from hundreds of people trampling it.

"Up for a ride on the Ferris wheel?" Ryan asked as they came to a stop.

She shook her head. "I'm scared to death of them. Anything but that."

"All right." The corner of his mouth quirked. "I take that to mean you don't mind going on other rides."

She returned his smile. "Well, maybe not *anything*."

CHAPTER 3

Megan and Ryan walked through the gate and into the melee of the carnival. As they strolled down the midway, brilliant colors, flashing lights, the shouts of carnies, and the clang and bang of games assaulted her senses. The crowd jostled them and it was almost too loud for them to hear each other talk.

Ryan took her by the hand, catching her off guard, and drew her out of the crowd. His hand was big and warm around hers as they came to a stop in front of the milk bottle game. To either side and across the top of the yellow and red striped awning hung stuffed brown monkeys and black gorillas of all sizes. The largest was a gorilla holding a half-peeled banana.

"Want to knock down a few bottles?" Ryan asked as he let Megan's hand slip from his.

"Sure." She smiled as she found herself wishing he were still holding her hand.

He dug in his pocket and pulled out a couple of ones and gave them to the carnie manning the game. The young man handed Ryan three balls.

"You first." Ryan gave one ball to Megan.

She took it, feeling a little self-conscious as she threw the ball. She missed the three metal milk bottles by a good six inches.

He smiled. "Give it another try."

She took another ball from Ryan and shook her head. "I never said I knew how to throw."

This time the ball brushed by one of the bottles, causing it to rock, but not enough to knock any of them down. She threw the third ball and missed the bottles entirely once again.

"Good try." Ryan handed the carnie more cash, and the young man in turn gave Ryan another three balls.

He set the balls on the wood barrier in front of them, then took one of the balls and pitched it hard at the milk bottles. The bottles scattered and she grinned up at him. He pitched the next two balls and nailed two more stacks of bottles, winning a small prize.

Instead of taking the prize, Ryan paid for more balls. He never missed and kept upgrading his prizes until he'd won the biggest prize, the huge gorilla with the banana. Megan hadn't realized a crowd had gathered until the people started applauding and congratulating Ryan.

The carnie took the gorilla down and gave the enormous stuffed animal to Ryan who in turn handed it to Megan.

She laughed as she embraced the gorilla. "No one has ever

won a stuffed animal for me before."

"I'll carry it for you." Ryan took the gorilla from her and held it under one arm.

"You must have been on your high school baseball team," she said as they moved past a crowded shooting gallery.

He gave a nod. "I was an outfielder."

"Baseball is one sport I actually like." She sidestepped an empty popcorn carton. "My favorite team has been the San Francisco Giants ever since I was a little girl and we saw a game when we visited the city."

"The Diamondbacks are my team," Ryan said. "I'm also a Dodgers fan from way back, before Arizona had a team."

"Looks like we've got a little competition already between us." She gave him a teasing look. "Considering both the Giants and the Diamondbacks are fighting for first place in the National League."

"We'll have to come up with a good wager," he said.

She raised her brows. "Now that's thinking ahead. The playoffs are almost a month from now and we've just met."

He shrugged. "I have a good feeling about you. My feelings are rarely wrong."

A tingling sensation went through her belly at the fact that he was thinking that far ahead and she'd just met him, and she couldn't think of anything to say.

He saved her by asking, "How about something to eat?"

In all of the fun spending time with Ryan, she'd forgotten she was hungry. "That sounds great."

He bought them corndogs and sodas, and a churro each. They continued talking as they walked and it wasn't long before the food was gone. When they finished, he bought a cone of cotton candy.

"No fair is complete without cotton candy," he said as he pulled at some of the pink and blue sticky stuff.

"What about siblings?" she asked.

He put it in his mouth. "Four brothers." Ryan crouched as a little boy ran straight toward him. "And a whole lot of cousins," he added before he caught the boy by the shoulders. "Hold on, pardner. Where's your mama?"

"Matt, I told you to stay with me." A pretty redheaded woman scooped the boy up into her arms. "Thank you, Ryan."

"Giving your mama a hard time?" Ryan straightened and tugged on the little boy's earlobe and the boy shook his head. To the woman Ryan said, "Carrie, this is Megan Wilder." He turned to Megan. "The ornery boy's mama is my cousin, Carrie Parks."

"Hi." Megan gave Carrie a smile.

The woman returned the smile. "Great to meet you." She turned to Ryan. "I've got to run. Jack has Cindy and they've been waiting for us by one of the ticket booths. Matt busted loose before we could get to them. I was afraid he'd manage to get lost in the middle of the crowd before I could stop him."

"We'll have to play ball sometime." Ryan ruffled Matt's hair before he looked up at the boy's mom. "See you around, Carrie."

As Carrie carried Matt away and vanished in the midst of the crowded carnival, Ryan and Megan continued walking along the midway to the closest ticket booth. He went up to the little window and purchased a handful of tickets from the carnie.

"Sure you don't want to go on the Ferris wheel?" Ryan said with a grin as he turned back to her.

Megan gave a big nod. "Absolutely positive."

"How about the Zipper?" He pointed toward the huge oblong

ride that turned and had baskets spinning all around it and people screaming with both laughter and terror. Amusement was in his gaze.

"Are you crazy?" She shook her head. "Nuh-uh. Nothing that turns upside down."

"The Tilt-a-Whirl." They stopped by the red spinning seats that looked like giant apples that went around in a big circle.

She bit the inside of her lip for a moment. "Okay. That one looks safe enough."

He took her hand and tugged her toward the ride. "Let's go."

They waited in line and he settled his arm around her shoulders. "Don't look so nervous."

"Ha." She met his gaze. "What if I throw up on you?"

"Lots of babies in the family so I'm used to it." He gave her a grin then nodded in the direction of two dunking booths. "If you do, we'll just have to get a little wet."

She laughed as she saw someone getting dunked. "Now that could be fun."

When it was their turn to get on the ride, they climbed into one of the huge apple-shaped seats and strapped in. There was a wheel in front of them.

"That makes it spin, doesn't it," she said dubiously.

"Yep." He grasped it. "Think you can handle it?"

"We'll find out." She held onto the wheel, too.

The ride started moving and Megan gasped as the apple started turning and gliding up and down. Ryan turned the wheel and the apple began spinning.

Megan squealed with laughter as she was thrown against Ryan from the force of the movement. Then he was sliding over her way, pinning her against the side of the apple. Back and forth they slid into each other and she found herself giggling so hard she was out of breath by the time the ride ended.

They climbed out of the ride when the apple came to a stop and she was a little wobbly on her feet. He took her hand and they walked down the steps to the gate that led outside of the ride's barrier.

Instead of another ride, they went through the House of Horrors. She couldn't help crying out the first time a creature jumped out and startled her, but then she found herself laughing with Ryan at the spook house's corny special effects.

Daylight waned and the carnival lights lit up the night. They headed away from the midway.

"There's a country western dance here at the fairgrounds tomorrow tonight," Ryan said as they walked toward the parking lot. "I'd like to take you."

They came to a stop beside her Toyota and she looked up at him. He was handsome in a sexy, hardworking cowboy kind of way. She'd enjoyed spending the afternoon and part of the evening with him, enjoyed it a lot.

She smiled. "I'd like that."

"Why don't I pick you up at seven for dinner?" he said. "I'll take you out for Mexican food and then the dance."

"I'll meet you there," she hurried to say. She wasn't ready to introduce him to her family. "Which restaurant?"

"Maria's," he said. "No better Mexican food in the southwest," he said.

She was glad he didn't pressure her to let him pick her up. "I'll be there at seven."

"All right," he said with a smile. "Are you sure you don't want me to pick you up?"

She nodded. "I have some things to take care of before dinner."

His voice was softer as he stepped in closer. "I'd like to kiss you good night, Megan."

Her belly flip-flopped. The way he was looking at her made her feel as if she was one of the hottest, sexiest women on earth.

She met his gaze, her breath coming faster and her throat suddenly dry. "I'd like that," she whispered.

He lowered his head, his mouth hovering over hers for a moment. Her heart rate picked up as he brushed his lips over hers. He pressed his mouth against hers and kissed her.

It was a slow, sensual kiss as his mouth moved over hers. When he drew away she wanted to grab him by the collar and yank him back toward her for a much longer kiss.

He brushed his thumb across her cheek. "What's your phone number?"

"I don't have any paper," she said.

He brushed a strand of hair from her face. "I'll remember it."

She had a hard time speaking but managed to stammer out her cell phone number.

"I'll see you tomorrow night," he said.

She nodded, having a hard time coming up with anything to say.

He waited until she was safely in her car and had started the vehicle before he walked away into the night.

CHAPTER 4

Megan shut the front door behind her with a solid thump as she entered her parents' home. She set down the stuffed gorilla that Ryan had won for her at the fair and smiled as she stroked its fur. What a fun day she'd had with the tall, dark, and handsome cowboy.

And he'd asked her out for tomorrow night. A sense of giddiness and excitement made her steps light as she turned and walked in the direction of the kitchen. It wasn't quite nine yet and she wondered if her parents were still up. Megan had considered changing her name back to Dyson from her married name, Wilder, but hadn't made the decision yet. She wanted to talk to her parents about it.

She heard her father's angry voice coming from the kitchen.

"Got another notice in the mail."

Megan frowned as she entered and saw both her parents looking upset.

Her mother, Margaret Dyson, was a tall, slender, striking woman who often reminded Megan of a TV mother from the fifties who always wore blouses, skirts, and heels. At least she didn't wear pearls, too.

Margaret carried a chocolate Bundt cake to the table. The kitchen smelled of warm cake that made Megan's mouth water.

"Wasn't his coming by the restaurant today enough?" Margaret was saying. "What does the notice say?"

Paul Dyson, a balding man, stared at the folded paper he was holding and adjusted his glasses. "It says exactly what he told us. If we don't make the payment by the next week, he's going to start foreclosure proceedings."

Margaret's lips tightened as she set the cake on the table. "It's not right. Not right at all."

"Foreclosure?" Megan said with surprise. "Is everything all right?"

Margaret glanced at the kitchen doorway and saw Megan. "Have some cake, Megan."

"I ate at the fair," Megan said.

"You should watch what you eat, anyway." Margaret looked disapprovingly at Megan. "You'll never catch and keep a decent man if you don't slim down. That Bart Wilder was not a decent man."

The back of Megan's neck burned. Her mother's remarks had always hurt, but it was the way she'd been as long as Megan could remember. Her father could be just as cutting in his own way, so it hadn't been easy growing up in the Dyson household. She was looking forward to moving back out on her own

"Margaret, it's too soon after her divorce for Megan to be looking for a man." Paul glanced at Megan. "God is not pleased when a man and woman are married before Him and they so lightly tear apart the sanctity of the union."

Even though she wanted to defend herself, Megan chose to ignore the remarks, pulled a chair up to the table, and sat near her father. "What's going on?"

Margaret set out two plates and forks on the table as Paul clenched the letter tighter. "A balloon payment is past due on the house," he said. "The owner won't work with us and we don't have the cash. Everything we have is sunk into the restaurant."

Megan's jaw dropped. "You could lose the house?"

"Yes," Margaret said as she started slicing into the cake.

Paul's skin had taken on a ruddy hue and he rubbed his chest, appearing agitated. "We've asked the owner to work with us but he's refused and is insisting on the whole amount."

Megan squeezed her hand shut on the tabletop. "How much is it?"

Paul's expression turned pained. "Twenty-five thousand," he said and Megan sucked in her breath.

"Everything that we didn't put into the restaurant we lost in the stock market," Margaret said. "We have nothing but the restaurant now and it's not bringing in enough."

Megan let out her breath. "I wish I had the money to help. With the economy being so bad I used up most of my savings over the past couple of years. What I had left is pretty much gone after the move here."

"Everything would have been perfectly fine if that Roger Meyer hadn't spread rumors about the restaurant and if some reporter hadn't written such a bad review. A false review. And then someone called the Health Department on us. Probably Meyer, too." Margaret moved a plate of cake in front of Paul and took one for herself, her words tight and angry. "First Meyer sets out to ruin us and now this."

Megan frowned. "Someone spread rumors?"

"He certainly did," Margaret said. "Mrs. Webb, Jenny's caregiver, overheard him one day, so we know it's true." Margaret's face was pinched as she went to the fridge and took out a carton of milk. She carried it to the table. "Some of what was said is that we've had roach problems which we have not. Among other things, someone reported that our hired help isn't legally in the U.S., which is also untrue. We think Meyer did that, too."

Paul's features turned darker. "After the rumors and the scathing review, business dropped off and never recovered."

Anger rose within Megan. "Who is this Roger Meyer?"

Margaret took two glasses out of the cabinet and poured a glass of milk for herself and one for Paul, then sat in the chair. "He owns a competing restaurant next door to ours. He leases that building from Mr. Cowell and wanted to lease our building, too, so that he could expand his place." She stabbed at her slice of cake. "He thought he had a deal worked out but we outbid him. He was angry. Met him one day and he said we would never make it and it would be a sorry day that we ever bought it."

Megan looked from her father to her mother and back. "Why didn't you tell me any of this before?"

"We'd hoped it wouldn't be an issue." Paul tossed the notice on the table and speared his cake with his fork as if driving it into an enemy. "If the owner gave us more time or let us work out some kind of payment plan, we might be able to make it. We put up seventy-five grand when we bought the place."

"He's going to keep our down payment and take everything away." Margaret's tone was bitter.

"What are you going to do?" Megan clenched her hands.

Paul swallowed a bite of cake and chased it down with milk before he spoke. "We'll give talking to him another try. If that doesn't work...I don't know what we'll do."

That the Hummingbird Café wasn't doing well was a shock to Megan. Her parents' restaurant was a family-style place, much like one they'd had in New Mexico before they'd moved to Prescott a year ago. Their restaurant in Albuquerque had been popular, successful, and profitable. Her mother's peach pie alone sold like crazy, not to mention her country potpies.

Megan spent a little more time with her parents as they told her about the reporter trashing the service as well as the food. The Health Department had come out and found nothing out of order, but damage was done by more rumors that were spread.

Also, on an Internet restaurant recommendation and review site, one negative review after another had been posted within a short timeframe. They were certain they were false reviews that had to be connected to Roger Meyer.

Her father changed the subject. "Why are you in so late tonight?"

"It's not that late." She glanced at the clock and saw that it was closing in on eleven, later than she'd thought it was. "Besides, we've been talking for a while."

"I found a home for you to buy," Paul said in his I've-decided-so-this-is-how-it's-going-to-be tone. "It's in this neighborhood. We can go look at it tomorrow."

"I'm not sure where I want to live yet," Megan said calmly. But she knew it wasn't going to be this close to her parents. She loved them, but she needed her space.

Paul finished his cake and wiped his hands on a napkin. "I know what's best, Megan. We've been here longer than you and I've already checked out all of the good neighborhoods. This is one you can afford and you'll be close to your mother."

Megan swallowed down the words she wanted to say. She stayed calm. "Dad, I'm thirty-two years old. I can handle it on my own."

Paul snorted.

Megan felt her face warm. "Time for me to get to bed." She said goodnight to her parents and retreated to the guest room.

"Why am I doing this?" she said to herself when she closed the door behind her. "Why did I come to Prescott? I feel like I'm sixteen again."

Megan fumed for a bit and then went to bed. Her thoughts bounced from her parents' financial difficulties to the way her father still tried to dominate her life to her evening with Ryan.

It didn't do her any good to worry over the restaurant and house tonight, so she settled on thinking about Ryan and the time they'd spent together.

Her lips tingled as she remembered his kiss and she brought her fingers to them. His kiss had been just enough to make her want more, yet she'd only met him today. With his long legs and taut muscular body, he was one tall, sexy cowboy.

She thought about the way his denim blue eyes had watched her all afternoon and the sensual curve of his smile. He'd made her feel sexy and beautiful in a way no man had ever made her feel before.

Thoughts of her ex-husband intruded, darkening everything. He'd taught her that a man wasn't always what he appeared to be on the surface. He'd made it clear she wasn't desirable to him any longer and it had made her wonder if she could be desirable to any man.

She frowned at her turn of thoughts. Bart Wilder had hurt her in ways no one ever had before. She wasn't going to let him take away the happiness she'd experienced today and the possibility that a man could find her attractive just the way she was.

A car passed by and light chased shadows on her walls. For too long she'd let Bart control her life and joy. That wasn't going to happen anymore.

She let her thoughts drift back to Ryan. She remembered his boyish grin when he'd won the gorilla and had presented her with it. Was she fooling herself by being so certain that Ryan was exactly who he said he was? She was sure he wasn't pretending to be someone he wasn't. She'd seen it in the way he'd interacted with children and adults alike, and by how popular he clearly was.

He seemed genuine and down to earth and a real man's man. He'd be tough when he needed to be or gentle when the situation called for it.

Was it possible he was thinking of her now, just as she was thinking about him?

She closed her eyes and gradually drifted off to sleep, dreaming of cowboys, gorillas, and banana peels.

CHAPTER 5

The sun was rising as Ryan went about his morning chores. The morning was clear, the sky a crystal blue, the cool air still.

He whistled to Ossie, his Australian shepherd, as he thought about the sexy brunette he'd spent the afternoon with yesterday. She had wide glass-green eyes framed with dark lashes and a smile that made something twist deep in his gut. He loved how her cute ass looked in her jeans. He wanted to run his hands along every one of her curves and to feel her warm, soft body against his.

She had a beautiful smile and a glow about her that told him she enjoyed life. Yet there was the hint of sadness in her eyes that made him want to protect her, to take whatever pain she'd felt and make it vanish with the wind. The thought that anyone could have hurt her made him grit his teeth. He barely knew Megan, but he'd be happy to knock the shit out of any man who tried to hurt her. Or who had already hurt her.

Ryan shook his head. Damn but he had it bad for the woman. Real bad.

Ossie answered his whistle, bolting toward him, coming from the direction of the corral.

He rubbed behind the dog's ears as she looked up at him with her clear blue eyes. She was a blue merle with a mottled black, white, and gray coat.

Ryan patted her head before straightening. "What have you been up to?"

Ossie stepped back and gave a single bark in answer.

"Ah, you've been up to no good." Ryan clicked his tongue. "Come on, girl. We have work to do."

She moved to his right, a step behind him. Ryan headed for the barn where one of his two part-time ranch hands was mucking out a stall. The young man usually smiled and hummed as he worked, but today he was quiet, his expression serious.

Ryan pushed up the brim of his Stetson as he came up beside Bill. "How's your mama? Is she out of the hospital yet?"

The usually upbeat young man faced Ryan and leaned on his shovel. "She's out of the hospital but she's not doing so good." He swallowed, his Adam's apple bobbing. "The doctor said Mama's got cancer and she doesn't have any insurance. I'm trying to get enough money together to help her buy groceries and pay her bills since she hasn't been able to work."

"Damn." Ryan felt like he'd taken a kick to his gut as he rested his hand on Bill's shoulder. He'd known Mary Jane Dow from the time they were kids. She'd gotten pregnant with Bill not long after they graduated from high school, some eighteen years ago, and had raised the boy on her own. "How much does she need?"

Bill took off his green John Deere cap, his blond hair damp from perspiration. He wiped sweat from his forehead with the back of his hand. "I've got part of it, but I need to make at least another thousand. I just don't know how I'm going to get everything she needs." He glanced at the ground then looked at Ryan again. "I need a second job to keep up with the bills."

Ryan nodded. "I'll ask around, see if anyone needs an extra hand."

"Thank you, sir." Bill's expression showed some relief. "I appreciate that."

The young man put his ball cap back on and turned back to work. Ryan headed to his home with Ossie at his side.

His boots thumped on the wood floor as he walked in the front door. Ossie's toenails clicked on the floor as she headed to the kitchen for a drink.

Ryan went through the house to the office just down the hall from the living room. He sat behind his scarred old desk that had been his granddaddy's, reached into one of the drawers, and drew out his checkbook. He picked up a pen and wrote out a check before he folded it and slid it into his shirt pocket.

When he finished, he pulled his cell phone from the leather holster on his belt and called his sister-in-law, Danica. She and Creed had married a year ago and he enjoyed her company. Hell, all of his brothers loved Danica.

"Hi, Ryan," she answered, obviously having seen his name come up on her phone's display. "How's it going?"

"Good." He liked the sound of Danica's voice. She always

sounded upbeat and in a positive mood. "Are you still looking for a little help around the place?" he asked.

"We could use another hand when Creed's on the road," Danica said. "And if he's good we might keep him on indefinitely. Do you have someone in mind?"

"Bill Dow is my part-timer and his mama has cancer," Ryan said. "I'm not sure you've had a chance to meet Mary Jane yet, but Bill needs to make extra cash to help her out. He's a hard worker and a good kid."

"I haven't met Mary Jane and I'm sorry to hear she's ill." Danica sounded concerned. "Go ahead and send Bill my way. Creed isn't going to be around a whole lot these next few months, so I'm sure I can put Bill to work."

"You've got it," Ryan said. "Thank you for giving him the opportunity."

"No problem." He heard the smile in her voice. "No doubt I'll be thanking you for referring him."

Ryan said goodbye and disconnected the call. He wrote Danica's cell phone number on a scrap of paper. He whistled to Ossie who came right to him before they headed out the door.

When Ryan returned to the barn, Bill was brushing down one of the horses. Ryan drew the check out of his shirt pocket and handed it to the young man.

Bill looked astonished as he stared at the check that was written out for a thousand dollars. He met Ryan's gaze. "Thank you, sir. I'll pay you back every cent."

"Consider it a bonus." Ryan pulled a pair of work gloves out of his back pocket and slipped them on. "You're a hard worker and you've earned it. If you need anything else for your mama, let me know."

"I don't know how to thank you enough." Relief was in Bill's gaze, but he still looked worried.

"Another thing." Ryan handed Bill the scrap of paper with Danica's number on it. "My sister-in-law could use a little help. When you're finished up here, give her a call and set a time to get together with her. I know you'll do a real good job for her."

"Yes, sir!" Bill's face brightened.

"When you're finished brushing down Sammy, I have a few more chores for you," Ryan said.

Bill thanked Ryan again as he put the check and paper in his jeans pocket and went right back to brushing down the horse. He was already a hard worker but he seemed to double his efforts.

Ossie left to investigate the back of the barn as Ryan went to the tower of alfalfa hay. He grasped the baling wire of one bale, swung it down, and carried it to the stalls. He grabbed a pair of wire cutters off of a shelf and cut through the baling wire. Alfalfa dust floated in the air as he tossed flakes of hay to each horse.

He shook his head as he thought of Bill's mama. She was a good woman and it was a damned shame she had cancer. He hoped to hell she'd beat it.

Ryan handled a few more chores in the barn before saddling his Quarter horse, Laredo. His thoughts turned to Megan. He'd committed her phone number to memory and wondered if he should call her to make sure she wasn't going to back out on him. Naw. He doubted she would stand him up. She didn't seem like the kind of woman who would leave a man hanging like that.

She hadn't wanted him to pick her up from her home and he wondered why. He'd had a feeling that there was something she was keeping to herself that she wasn't ready to tell him. He hadn't pressed her. He was certain she'd let him in after she got to know him and knew she could trust him.

With Ossie at his side, he spent the day doing chores, including checking stock tanks and fence lines, and mending a fence that was down. Toward the end of the day, Laredo threw a shoe and he had to walk the mare back to the barn and re-shoe her.

By the time he was finished, the sun hung low in the sky. It had been a long day and he was ready for a night out with Megan. Just thinking about her made him smile.

He wasn't sure exactly what had captured his attention first. He'd watched her walk to the small arena where the 4-H'ers showed their livestock. The gentle sway of her hips as she walked had been enough to draw him closer. He'd paused to watch her before she looked at him and her cheeks had blushed a pretty pink. Damn, but she was sexy.

Spending the afternoon with her had just proven to him that she was a woman worth getting to know. He loved her smile and laughter. The way she'd giggled on the ride had been adorable.

Yeah, he was sure as hell looking forward to getting to know Megan Wilder a whole lot better.

CHAPTER 6

The clear Friday night was cooling off as Megan walked from the parking lot and around the back of Maria's restaurant. Megan wore a flowing denim skirt with boots and a western blouse, and her brown hair was pulled back in a French braid. The ground was rocky and uneven across the parking lot and she was glad for the boots rather than having worn something more delicate.

She had barely managed to slip out of the house without her parents grilling her on who she was meeting. She was thirty-two and her parents treated her like a teenager. As much as she loved them, they embarrassed her with the kinds of remarks they made around the men she met. She was going to have to move out soon if she was going to retain her sanity.

A tall figure emerged from the darkness just feet away from

her and her heart stuttered. The man looked intimidating with his powerful build and his features shadowed by his western hat.

She came to a complete stop as the man moved closer.

"Hi, Megan." Ryan stepped into the light, his lips curved into a smile. He wore a white western shirt with dark blue Wranglers, a big silver and gold belt buckle on his leather belt and polished boots that weren't scuffed and worn like the ones he'd worn yesterday.

"Ryan." She held her hand to her heart. "You scared me."

He reached her and tugged on the end of her braid that was lying over her shoulder. "I wouldn't want to do that." His voice was husky as his eyes met hers. "You look gorgeous."

"Thank you," she said as warmth flooded through her.

"Come on, sweetheart." He put his hand at the base of her spine and they walked toward the front of the building.

Smells of Mexican food drifted over her as they entered the restaurant that was dim but had brightly painted walls of blue, green, and pink. On the walls were serapes, maracas, sombreros, and other art depicting Hispanic culture. In a painting closest to the entrance, dancers in colorful traditional costume were performing a Mexican hat dance. In another painting, a matador held a red cape while a bull charged, the audience seated around him in a huge arena.

The restaurant's atmosphere was cozy. The hostess was beautiful with her hair pulled back and wore a white embroidered peasant blouse with a red embroidered fiesta skirt.

"Rosanne," Ryan said with a smile as he greeted the hostess. "How are you doing?"

Her smile was brilliant as she greeted him. "Very well, Señor McBride." Roseanne spoke with a strong Hispanic accent. She turned her gaze on Megan, still smiling. "Good evening, Señora."

Megan replied in kind and Roseanne asked if they were a party of two. Ryan gave a nod and the hostess picked up a couple of menus and indicated that they should follow her.

She showed them to a cozy corner table where Ryan seated Megan before taking his own seat beside her. Megan never realized how nice it was to have a man act like a gentleman. She was used to anything but gentlemen.

Ryan put his menu on the table. "You look beautiful." He trailed his fingers down her arm and their eyes locked.

Something about his expression made her think of a future with them together, beyond dating.

Warmth spread through her. She couldn't remove her gaze from his.

A server stopped by with a basket of tortilla chips, breaking the intensity of the moment.

Flushing, Megan reached for one of the chips and put it on her plate and tried to think of something to say. "They're still warm."

Now that was lame, Megan, she told herself.

"Do you want something hot to put on them?" He gestured to the salsa and hot sauce.

Ryan's easygoing manner set her at ease. She didn't feel like this was a first date, even though it technically was. They'd spent time at the fair together, but it hadn't been an official date since they'd only just met.

She ate a chip just as the waitress arrived. Like the hostess, the waitress wore a peasant blouse with an embroidered fiesta skirt. "Señor McBride, it is good to see you with us again."

"You know you can't keep me away." He nodded to Megan. "Gabriella, this is Megan." To Megan he said, "This is Gabriella, my favorite waitress."

"A pleasure, Señora." Gabriella gave a smile and a nod to Megan.

Megan smiled at Gabriella. "Likewise."

Megan said she wasn't crazy about beer and ordered a margarita over the rocks with salt on the rim. Ryan ordered a Tecate beer for himself.

"How do you like Prescott?" Ryan asked after Gabriella had left.

"So far so good," she said. "It's a lot smaller than I'm used to, but I think the slower paced lifestyle will suit me."

"You've come to the right place." He flashed a grin. "Were you born and raised in Albuquerque?"

She nodded. "I've never lived anywhere else until now." She tilted her head to the side. "Exactly where do you live?"

"Thirty minutes outside of Prescott," he said.

She raised her brows. "I didn't realize it was such a drive."

He shrugged. "Around here, that's nothing."

"I'd love to see your ranch sometime." Then her body heated as she realized that might have been too forward on a first date.

"I'd like that," he said. "If you don't mind making the drive."

She shook her head. "Like you said, thirty minutes isn't far."

"Just avoid speeding too much." He winked.

"I'll try," she said. "But my foot tends to get a little heavy at times."

"Watch out for John." Ryan looked amused. "He'd ticket his own brother."

With a laugh, she said, "I'll wait 'til I'm out of town."

Gabriella returned with the margarita for Megan and the beer for Ryan and asked them if they were ready to order. Megan went with her favorite, two cheese enchiladas, and Ryan chose a plate of tacos with shredded beef. Both plates would include refried beans and Spanish rice.

After the waitress left, Megan brought her margarita to her lips and tasted the salt along the rim as she sipped the tangy drink. Ryan took a swig of his beer then ate another chip as she set down her large glass.

"You mentioned you have cattle," she said. "How many?"

"Roughly forty head," he said.

"What kind?" She found herself exceedingly curious about Ryan.

"Angus," he said.

She grasped her margarita, feeling the coolness of the glass and the condensation beneath her fingers. "They're black, aren't they? I believe I remember that from the fair when you were showing me the livestock. Hereford are red with white faces and bellies and Brahma are white."

"Yep." He nodded. "You've got it right. Angus are solid black, although there might be a little white on a cow's udder."

She took a sip of her margarita. "How many Suffolk sheep do you have and what do you do with them?"

"About a dozen," he said. "I started raising Suffolk when I was a 4-H kid. I primarily breed champion stock for FFA and 4-H kids to raise, breed, show, and sell."

"FFA is Future Farmers of America, is that right?" she asked. "I think we had FFA in high school, but it's been so long ago and I had other interests."

"Yes." He raised his beer bottle. "I was in that organization in high school as well as continuing 4-H."

"How long have you been teaching 4-H'ers?" she asked.

"I was a member of the organization until I was nineteen, then went off to Northern Arizona University for four years and got my business degree. When I returned I was asked to help out and from that point on I've been a leader, roughly twelve years."

"No wonder you seemed to know every kid there," she said with a smile.

"Not to mention I grew up here." He gave her a quick grin. "Not a whole lot I don't know about the area and the people who've been here as long as I have."

"I've heard that a lot of people have started moving to the Prescott area to retire," she said, "or just to settle down where life is a little quieter and slower paced."

"That's exactly what they'll get here." He took a chip from the bowl at the center of the table. "Although I have to admit that I hope not too many people discover this part of the country. The population has gotten pretty darn big."

"I can understand that. It's a beautiful area." She watched him eat his chip, studying the strong lines of his features and the blue of his eyes. She swallowed. "So you have four brothers?"

He nodded. "One younger than me and three older. All of them also live around the valley, although Creed is on the road travelling the bull riding circuit a good portion of the time. I have at least a dozen cousins here and scattered around the state."

"I have a small family. Just my parents, my sister, and my niece." She hurried to move away from talk about her family. "Is your family close?"

"Most of us." Ryan nodded. "My brothers and I fought grow-ing up but we get along pretty well now. What about you and your sister?"

"Tess is older than me by five years, so I think I drove her crazy following her around when I was little." Megan smiled. "But we've always been close. She and her daughter mean the world to me."

Ryan swallowed down more of his drink then lowered his bottle "Where did you go to school?"

"The University of New Mexico." She pushed a strand of hair behind her ear. "I majored in English but ended up in graphic de-sign."

She only had one margarita since she'd be driving but the one she did have helped her to relax into the conversation. Their food arrived while they fell into a discussion about baseball.

Dinner was delicious but there was so much food that she only managed to eat a little over half of her plate. Ryan cleared his plate and ate more chips on top of that.

When they were ready to go, Ryan paid the bill and then put his hand at her elbow while he escorted her out of the restaurant.

As they walked outside, Megan heard two men shouting from the direction of the parking lot. Ryan came to a stop and looked down at her, his expression grim as the men's voices escalated. "Wait here."

She frowned as he walked away from her and rounded the restaurant toward the parking lot. She followed him and stood at the corner of the building.

Two men were standing in the middle of the lot, shouting at

each other.

"You sonofabitch," a man in a black western hat was saying. "You stole my girl. I'm gonna kick your ass."

A smaller man raised his hands and balled them into fists. "Marnie wasn't yours, you dumb shit. She can't even stand the sight of you."

"Ron, settle down." Ryan stepped closer to the men. "You don't want to do this."

"Shut up, McBride." The man named Ron slurred the words.

Great, Megan thought. The man was drunk.

"Why don't you get on out of here, Dave," Ryan said to the other man. "No sense in this turning ugly."

Dave was a young wiry man who didn't look strong enough to fight Ron. Dave spit onto the dirt. "He's not going to hurt me. He's so shitfaced he wouldn't be able to hit the side of a barn if it was right in front of him."

Ron made a roaring sound and charged Dave. Ryan grabbed onto Ron and gritted his teeth as he held the man back. Ryan's muscles bulged and it was clear that it was an effort to hold on.

"You're bigger than he is, Ron, and you were in the military." Ryan hung on. "It wouldn't be a fair fight."

Megan's heart pounded as Ron turned and swung at Ryan.

Ryan dodged the blow then shoved Ron away from him. "I know you're spoiling for a fight, but you don't want to mess with me."

"You think you're so damned tough, don't you," Ron snarled. "All of you McBrides are nothing but a bunch of piss ants."

Ryan didn't appear like the remark bothered him at all. "Let's all just go on home. Enough is enough."

Ron charged Ryan who swept out one boot and knocked Ron's feet out from under him. Ron hit the ground hard but scrambled up, his fists raised.

"I'm not going to hurt you," Ryan said, his voice still calm. "But I will put an end to this."

Ron growled and charged Ryan again. Ryan dodged out of the way and the drunken man stumbled past Ryan and hit the dirt face first.

Flashing red and blue lights illuminated the scene as a police cruiser pulled up. Two officers exited the car and walked toward them as Ron staggered to his feet.

"What's going on?" one of the officers asked.

"Ron's had too much to drink and he was spoiling for a fight with Dave Turner," Ryan said.

"That wouldn't have been a fair fight, now would it, Ron," one officer stated as he dragged Ron to his feet.

Megan noticed a small crowd had gathered. One of the men stepped in and explained how Ryan tried to stop the fight and how Ron had tried to assault him.

By the time everything was straightened out, Ron was in the back of the cruiser and the crowd had broken up.

Ryan returned to Megan. "Sorry about that," he said. "I just didn't want to see anyone get hurt."

"No apologies necessary." She shook her head. "I'm just glad you didn't end up getting hurt."

He settled his hand on her shoulder. "Ready to head on out to the dance?"

She let out her breath, glad everything had turned out all right. "That sounds like a really good idea to me."

"Why don't you leave your car here at the restaurant and ride with me?" he asked. "I'll bring you back here after the dance."

"All right." She fell into step beside him as he walked toward a silver truck.

His truck was high off the ground. She stepped onto the runner, then climbed into the truck with his help, and he closed the door behind her.

He drove the vehicle through a rural area to get to the fairgrounds and she held her hands in her lap. Part of her felt comfortable with him and another part was nervous. So far the night had been wonderful. If you didn't count the scuffle outside the restaurant.

The truck started rattling and thumping, jostling them in the truck cab.

"Damn." Ryan glanced at Megan as he started to pull the truck to the side of the road. "I think the truck has a flat. Must have picked up a nail."

When the truck was on the shoulder, he parked then hopped out to check the tire before he returned. "Yep," he said. "It's flat all right. Shouldn't take too long to change it."

She started to climb out and then he was there and helped her down onto the shoulder that had a bit of a drop off a couple of feet from the truck. He took off his hat and started to unbutton his shirt. She watched as he removed it and found herself disappointed that he was wearing a T-shirt beneath it. She'd been hoping for some fine naked male torso.

The flat was on the driver's side and as she watched he removed the spare from beneath the vehicle. Black smudged his T-shirt as he brought out the tire. He grabbed a jack and tire iron out of the truck before popping off the hubcap and removing the lug nuts with the tire iron.

She eased down beside him. "Anything I can do?"

"I've got it." He met her gaze. "You can just sit there looking pretty."

A burst of heat went through her as he looked at her and then he returned to changing the tire.

When he finished, he stood and wiped down his hands with a rag he'd taken out of one of the truck's toolboxes.

She looked up at the zillions of stars overhead. "Nice night for a flat."

He tossed the rag into the toolbox. "It gave me more alone time with you." He moved closer to her and when her gaze met his, he brushed her cheek with his thumb. "I don't know how you ended up with a smudge, but you have one right there," he murmured. "You're even more beautiful with a little mess."

Her lips parted as she looked into his eyes while he lowered his head and his mouth met hers. She gave a soft moan as his kiss deepened and she grasped his biceps, holding on as if she might fall. His kiss made her knees feel weak as he settled his hands on her hips.

She felt as if everything was starting to spiral out of control as their kisses grew hungrier, needier.

And then he was pulling away from her. She looked into his eyes, which glittered in the darkness.

"We'd better get to the dance," he murmured as he gently stroked a loose strand of hair from her face. "I have to admit there are other places I'd like to take you to right now rather than dancing where I might have to share you with someone else."

She felt herself blush and was glad for the darkness. She tried to speak lightly as she said, "I don't think you'll have to worry about that."

"I don't intend to let anyone cut in," he said. "As far as I'm concerned, you're mine for the night."

CHAPTER 7

Megan and Ryan walked toward the building where the county fair's dance was being held. The carnival rose up behind the fair buildings and lit up the darkness with its colorful blinking lights. Country-western music floated through the night.

She liked the feel of his big hand around hers, strong and callused. He smiled down at her and squeezed her hand.

They rounded a corner and stepped into the glow outside the large building's front doors. Light spilled out of the opening onto the ground and over couples standing outside and talking. The music was loud and energetic and through the doors Megan could see dancers two-stepping to a song the band was playing.

Ryan was greeted as soon as they walked out of the shadows and he introduced her to people he knew.

The women wore tight cowgirl jeans and two of them wore western hats. Megan found herself feeling a little self-conscious with so many slender women around her. Here she was with her full curves and an incredibly good-looking man who seemed to be well known and popular wherever he went.

The two men Megan met were polite and friendly and shook her hand. One of the women Ryan knew was just as friendly but another was more reserved.

A third woman, who wore a tight little skirt, a skimpy top, and had long blonde-streaked hair, went up to Ryan, ignoring Megan. "Hi, Ryan," she said with a flirtatious smile.

"Hi, Marnie." Ryan said, and Megan wondered if Marnie was the same woman Ron and Dave were fighting over. One of them had said her name. Ryan started to say something else, but Marnie went on.

"It's been a long time since we've gotten together." Marnie glanced at Megan and looked her up and down with a look that said "What are you doing with *her?*" Out loud, Marnie said, "Is this one of your cousins?"

"This is my date, Megan Wilder." Ryan rested his hand at Megan's waist and he looked at her as he nodded toward the other woman. "Megan, this is Marnie Timmons."

"One of Ryan's old girlfriends," Marnie said to Megan before turning back to Ryan. "Why don't we get together sometime?"

Megan's face heated. It was clear the woman was doing this to make Megan feel insecure.

"I'm kind of busy. I'll see you around, Marnie," he said politely before turning toward the dancehall's doors with his hand still at Megan's waist.

Megan swore she could feel Marnie's eyes boring into her back as they walked away.

Ryan leaned down and spoke close to Megan's ear. "I dated Marnie a couple of times in high school. She was never actually my girlfriend."

Just as they moved toward the entrance, another couple greeted them. It was the police officer who'd stopped her before and he was with a pretty, petite woman.

"Megan, I believe you've met my cousin, Officer John Mc-Bride," Ryan said. "This is his girlfriend, Sheri." He turned to the couple. "John, Sheri, this is Megan Wilder."

John extended his hand. "I stopped you outside of Prescott, Ms. Wilder. You have something of a lead foot."

"Call me Megan." She smiled at Ryan's cousin. "I'm working on being a totally law abiding citizen in your city."

He laughed. "I've got my eye on you."

Megan took Sheri's hand and the petite woman smiled. "Nice to meet you," Sheri said and Megan responded in kind.

"We'll see you inside," Ryan said.

Ryan and Megan walked into the dancehall that was decorated with red, white, and blue streamers, banners, and balloons. Tables to the left of the dance area were loaded with two large rectangular cakes and big bowls of punch. People stood on the outskirts of the dance floor and talked while couples two-stepped to a fast paced song.

"Would you like a little punch?" Ryan asked over the music.

"Sure." Megan smiled as he took her hand and they walked to a table with two clear punchbowls filled with the red drink.

He ladled punch into a couple of paper cups and handed one

to her. "Ready for a piece of cake?"

Megan took the punch and shook her head. "Maybe later." They moved from the table and Ryan guided her away from the crowd. After she took a drink of punch she met his gaze. "I have to make a confession."

He raised an eyebrow. "Shoot."

"I can't dance worth beans." She gave a nod toward the dance floor. "I'm afraid my feet will get tangled with yours if I try that."

"You can step on my boots all you want," he said with a grin as a new tune started up. "If you're finished with your punch we can start your lesson now."

"You asked for it," she said as he took her empty paper cup and tossed it along with his into the closest trashcan.

A fluttery feeling went through her belly as they moved out onto the dance floor. He started by showing her how to dance a country waltz to the slower paced song that was playing.

She followed his lead and managed to step on his boots only a few times before she got into the dance. She found herself laughing as he spun her around and brought her back to him. A fast-paced tune started up and the next thing she knew he was showing her how to two-step. She caught on faster than she'd expected.

Like Ryan had predicted, two men tried to cut in but he refused to let go of her.

By the time they'd danced to four songs, she was out of breath. She was about to tell Ryan she was ready for a break when the band started playing a slow song.

Ryan drew her into his arms, his warm body close to hers. "You're a fast learner," he said as he smiled down at her.

She shook her head and laughed. "You're being kind."

"I'm serious." He moved her around the dance floor. "You only stepped on my boots a couple dozen times."

With a grin she said, "Are you sure that was all?"

"Do you drive as fast as you learn to dance?" he said in a teasing tone.

Her lips twisted with amusement. "I must say, I don't move as fast as you."

"Oh, so you think I've been speeding with you," he said.

"You might have been speeding," she said, "but there's something about a nice exterior, pretty blue headlights and a nice rear end, moving fast."

He burst out laughing. "So you think I have a nice bumper?"

"No doubt about it." She was surprised at how easy it was to joke around with him.

He swung her around, catching her off guard and causing her to clutch his shoulders. She giggled as he brought her into his arms again as the song came to an end.

With a grin he said, "If I'm not mistaken, I think you're encouraging me to move faster."

She managed to hold back another laugh. "Well, let's just say I would not give you a citation for that."

A country line dance started almost immediately, the floor filling with dancers.

"Let's skip the line dance," she said and they moved away from the dance floor.

"Fine by me." He took her hand and squeezed it. "Never could get into it."

As they walked away from the dancers, they bumped into more people Ryan knew. He introduced Megan and they chatted for a few moments before moving on.

Just as they moved away from a couple, they stopped in front of a man who was standing and watching the dance floor with his shoulder hitched up against a wall.

Ryan introduced the man as his brother, Tate, and Megan shook hands with him. Tate was tall like Ryan, but had green eyes and harder features. He was friendly with a sexy little smile but seemed to be a little more reserved than Ryan.

"Megan is new to Prescott," Ryan said as Tate released Megan's hand.

"Did you move here permanently?" Tate asked in a low drawl. His eyes showed that he was genuinely interested.

She nodded. "That's the plan."

"What do you do?" he asked.

"I'm a graphic designer. Everything from websites, to brochures, to advertisements," she said.

He looked interested. "Might need your number. It's about time I set up a website for my business."

She smiled. "I'd love to talk with you whenever you decide you're ready."

"I have Megan's number," Ryan said. "I'll get it to you."

When they finished talking with Tate, Ryan said, "Let's get out of here." He put his hand at the base of her spine and guided her toward the back of the room. He opened a door and they stepped into the near darkness not lit up by the dancehall lights. Perspiration at her nape and on the rest of her exposed skin cooled in the night air.

"All that dancing makes for a great workout," she said as he closed the door behind them and they moved away from it.

He rested his hands at her waist, just above the flare of her hips as his gaze met hers. Heat spread from where he touched her, moving up to her breasts and down to her thighs.

She bit the inside of her lip as a rush of emotion traveled through her. What was she doing? She shouldn't let someone in like this, not this fast. She barely knew him but she felt something about him take hold of her heart. It was crazy and far too soon.

He lowered his head, bringing his mouth toward hers. Her heart pounded faster and her breath caught in her throat. His breath was warm on her lips a moment before he kissed her.

His kiss turned from gentle to passionate, all fire and need.

Without truly being conscious of what she was doing, she slipped her arms around his neck and kissed him back. The kiss was deeper than the one last night and when he drew away she found herself breathing heavier again, as if she'd just finished another dance.

His look was intense, almost serious, as he brushed his knuckles along her cheekbone. "Is it too soon to ask if you'd like to go camping with me next weekend?"

Her lips parted in surprise. "Alone?"

"I promise to be a gentleman." He moved his hands to her waist again. "Two sleeping bags and two tents."

"That's no fun," she said with a flirty smile. "Besides, I am afraid of being alone in the dark. And bears. I'm definitely afraid of bears."

He laughed. "I actually have a bear-proof camper trailer that we can take. Separate bunks even."

"Bear-proof, huh?" She tilted her head to the side as she considered it. Why not? She was certain she'd have a good time with

Ryan.

"Okay," she said. "It sounds like fun."

"I'd like to see you this week," he said, "But I have to go out of town until next Thursday night. How about I pick you up early Friday morning? Can you take off a Friday?"

Mild disappointment slid through her veins that she wouldn't see him until the following Friday while at the same time excitement over the camping trip made her smile. "My schedule is my own. I can meet you at your ranch and if it's okay with you, I can leave my car there until we get back."

"That works." He took both her hands in his. "Are you ready to head back inside?"

She nodded. "I could use another cup of punch."

"You've got it." He escorted her back into the building and they slipped into the crowd.

He kept his hand at her waist. It seemed a bit possessive like he wanted everyone to know she was with him. She liked that thought, that he wanted her to belong with him.

As he got them more punch, along with pieces of cake, she wondered at her thoughts. She'd known the man for two days but her heart seemed to be racing right along, speeding the same way she liked to drive.

She watched him as he ladled punch into cups. Was she crazy for going camping with him so soon after meeting him? Mentally, she shrugged. It would be a great opportunity to get to know him better and she had no doubt that he'd be a lot of fun to spend a weekend with.

And deep inside she trusted him. Something told her that he wouldn't pressure her for more than she was willing to give.

When he returned they found a couple of unoccupied chairs and ate pieces of white cake with buttercream frosting. An American flag had decorated the cake and Megan's piece was frosted blue with a white star in the middle of it.

She bit into the cake, which had a custard filling and was delicious. After a few bites, she looked at Ryan and saw that he was watching her and smiling. "You have blue from the frosting on your lips."

"Oops," she said and started to bring a napkin to her mouth.

"Let me," he said and brought his mouth to hers. He slowly kissed her, running his tongue along her lips. He raised his head and looked at her mouth. "There. You're blue-free."

"Are you sure?" she said and he grinned and kissed her again.

After the kisses, they did the best they could to talk over the loud music, but it wasn't easy. When they finished eating they moved out to the dance floor and fell into another country waltz.

Megan felt almost high as she danced with Ryan. She hadn't felt this happy in a long time. A really long time.

She was out of breath when they stopped for a break and Ryan grabbed two more cups of punch, handing her one. As they were walking away from the punch and cake table, Ryan gestured with his cup toward a man and a woman across the room.

"That's my brother, Gage, with the brunette." He looked at Megan. "I'd like you to meet him."

"I'd love to meet another one of your brothers," she said.

Ryan rested his hand at the base of her spine as they walked toward Gage. When they reached him and the brunette woman, Ryan introduced them.

"Gage, Chloe, this is my date, Megan Wilder." He turned to

Megan. "Gage and his girlfriend, Chloe."

Gage shook Megan's hand. "Nice to meet you, Megan." Gage was tall and muscular with dark hair, green eyes and she liked the sound of his voice. The cowboy was so sexy that she was certain he had plenty of women chasing him.

Chloe took Megan's hand but looked wary, as if Megan might try to steal Gage from her. As cute as the petite brunette was, Megan couldn't begin to believe that could happen, even if she tried.

Another man walked up holding a cup of punch in his hand. Ryan introduced the man as Blake, the oldest McBride brother.

Tall, dark, and dangerous looking, Blake had a hard look to him, and as she shook his hand, Megan could tell he was a man of few words.

"You've met all of my brothers with the exception of Creed," Ryan said as they walked away. "He's on the road in the bull riding circuit."

Toward the end of the evening, when Megan's feet were sore, Ryan took her hand and they walked outside. The night was cool and beautiful.

"I'm not ready for the night to end," he said as his gaze met hers. "What do you say we go for a little drive?"

"All right." She wasn't ready for the night to end, either.

After they went to his truck and he helped her climb in, they headed out. He drove up Senator Highway north out of Prescott until they came to a lookout where they could see the city spread out before them, lights twinkling in the night.

Ryan backed the truck up and they got out and sat on the tailgate, close to each other. It was peaceful and quiet. Magical.

He settled his arm around her shoulders and she rested her

head on his muscular arm. "It's beautiful here," she said, her voice breaking the quiet of the night.

"You're beautiful, Meg," he said.

She tilted her face to look up at him. He raised his hand and touched the side of her face. "I want to kiss you again," he said softly.

"I want that, too." Her voice came out in a whisper.

He lowered his head and then his mouth was firm against hers. He caught the end of her braid in his hand and she realized he had pulled off the clip and was unraveling the French braid as he kissed her.

His kiss was powerful but sensual as he slipped his fingers into her dark silky hair and he cupped the back of her head.

She slid her hands up his chest to his neck and held on as he kissed her until her mind spun. She couldn't think straight as he tasted her and made her hungry for him in ways she'd never thought possible.

When he drew away, she met his gaze and saw his eyes glittering in the darkness. He ran his thumb along her lower lip. "Even though I don't want this night to end," he said. "I'd better get you back to your car at the restaurant before we end up staying here a whole lot longer."

CHAPTER 8

Sunday morning, Megan studied her laptop screen as she worked to update a client's website. Even though Sunday was a day she usually took off, she had to get the updates done and then immediately start working on a new client's website.

Her mind kept wandering to Ryan and the fantastic time they'd had at the dance Friday night and later when they were looking over the city. She normally could do website updates blindfolded, but today her lack of concentration was going to get her in trouble.

Images of his sexy grin made her smile. He was so dang good looking. As far as she was concerned, he wasn't just eye candy or eye broccoli. He could easily be a complete meal topped with dessert.

When she messed up the updates for the third time, she groaned and put her head on her arms on the desk. She needed to get her act together and she needed to do it now. It was stupid to feel like a lovesick teenager at her age.

She raised her head and leaned back in her chair in front of the desk in her parents' guestroom. If she didn't have such a tight deadline for the updates as well as the website she'd promised to have up and running this week, she'd go out and start looking for a house now. She pushed hair out of her face. Maybe since she couldn't get her act together she'd go look anyway, then put in time 'til late tonight.

With a sigh, she stared out the window and watched sunlight winking through leaves of the tree that shaded that side of the house. She hadn't heard from Ryan yesterday, but she wasn't surprised since he'd left town to catch a flight from Phoenix to Montana to go to his cousin's wedding. Apparently they were having a Sunday afternoon wedding because the church hadn't been available at all on Saturday and not until Sunday afternoon. Ryan had told her the date held significance for the bride and groom and they were determined to have their wedding on that date.

Her thoughts turned to the possibility that her parents could be losing their home and she wondered if they were going to make it. She frowned as she thought about what they'd told her—a man was setting out to destroy the reputation of the Hummingbird Café and put her parents out of business.

Was there anything she could do to help them save their house and their business?

Megan let the thoughts turn in her mind, trying to think of some way to help. She pulled her hair back and fastened it with a band that had been sitting beside the computer then clicked a new tab on the Internet browser and did a search for Prescott area rental homes. She intended to rent for a while before finding a home to buy.

After she put in her criteria, she found three homes she was interested in and wrote down the telephone numbers and contacts. She wanted a fairly small place with three bedrooms or two bedrooms and a den; two baths; no pool; and desert landscaping that didn't require much in the way of maintenance. She doubted there were many pools in Prescott, but it was still one of her must-not-haves.

Just as she reached for her cell phone to call the first contact, her phone rang. She looked at the caller identification screen and saw that it was Bart's mother.

Her skin tingled as mixed feelings went through her. She loved Bart's family, she just didn't love Bart. She missed Grace and Montgomery Wilder, Bart's parents.

Megan took a deep breath and answered. "Hi, Grace."

"Megan," Grace said. "It's good to hear your voice."

"It's good to hear yours, too," Megan said and meant it. "How are you?"

"Lovely, Megan." Grace was a refined, educated woman with a pleasant speaking voice. "Are you doing well these days?"

Megan shifted the phone to her opposite ear. "I just moved to Prescott recently."

"That's why I'm calling," Grace said. "Bart told me you've moved and I need your address."

"I can give you my parents' address," Megan said. "I'm still looking for a place of my own."

"We miss you, Megan," Grace said quietly.

"I miss all of you too." Megan felt like a large rubber ball was lodged in her throat and she tried to keep the tears she felt out of her voice. "I'm sorry I went underground. It's just been…difficult."

"Oh, honey." Grace sighed. "You have nothing to be sorry for. In fact, I'm sorry for the way Bart treated you and that he was such an ass."

A tear rolled down Megan's cheek. She hated that she still got emotional despite the fact that it had been seven months since Bart had left her for another woman.

"You've been nothing but great." Megan swallowed hard. "Thank you."

"You are a wonderful woman, Megan."

"So are you, Grace." Megan sniffed back another tear. "You said you need my address?"

There was a shuffle of papers on the other end of the line. "Christine is getting married to a fine young man named Todd, and we would like to invite you to the wedding."

"Tell her congratulations, please." Megan pictured Bart's beautiful and sweet younger sister. "I would love to go," she added, "But I don't think I could handle it just yet. It's so hard for me to think you're not my mother-in-law and I'm not family anymore. It would just be too difficult."

"Megan, nothing has changed between you and the rest of the family," Grace said. "We miss you and want you to feel comfortable if you visit, which we hope you will. We still think of you as the same wonderful sweet person you have always been. Every member of the family is angry with Bart for what he did and we feel nothing but love and sadness for you."

"Thank you," Megan said.

Grace continued, "We understand that you need your space, but we want you to know you're a part of this family and always will be. And that goes for any man you might meet and marry someday. This family knows what happened to you. You are deserving of the best and we want the best for you. The rest of the family has given you space because you've said you needed that. They just want you to be happy."

Megan was so choked up she could barely speak. "What you just said means more to me than you know, Grace."

"I meant every word," Grace said. "If you change your mind, we would love to see you. It's been too long."

Megan took a deep breath as she tried to gather herself. "I miss our lunches." In the past, Megan and Grace would join each other for lunch once a month. Once Bart had left her, it was just too awkward for Megan.

"I miss them, too, honey," Grace said. "If you decide to come to the wedding you could stay longer, and we could do breakfast or lunch once the kids are off on their honeymoon."

"I'd like that, and I'll think about it," Megan said. "Are you ready to take down my parents' address?"

"Just a second…" Grace trailed off. "Now I am."

Megan spelled out the street name as she gave Grace the address.

"If it works out that you can come, feel free to bring a guest with you," Grace said.

Despite the fact that she barely knew him, Megan thought about how much fun it would be if Ryan went with her. All the way to Albuquerque? She shook her head at her thought. But it was a really nice thought.

"Thanks, Grace," Megan said. "Please give Montgomery a hug for me."

"I will do that," Grace said. "I hope we can get together soon."

Tears pricked at the back of Megan's eyes. "Someday we will." One of the hardest parts of the divorce was the fact that she wouldn't get to see Bart's family regularly like she used to. It had just been too difficult emotionally.

When they disconnected the call, Megan took a deep breath.

And then it hit her again. All of it. The pain of Bart's betrayal, his verbal abuse, the way he'd left her—it slammed into her with such force that tears started rolling down her cheeks. She held her hand to her mouth, holding back a sob.

When she was first married, she'd imagined a perfect little life. A nice house, two or three children, and a husband who loved her.

Now she was divorced with no children. She missed her ex's family terribly. It was like all of her dreams had been smashed into bits.

A tissue box sat on the corner of her desk and she grabbed a tissue and pressed it to her face as she cried.

Before they were married, she should have seen the signs, but she'd either missed them or overlooked them. A few months after they were married, he began acting domineering, stayed out late, spent time with his friends instead of her, and then the verbal abuse started.

She thought that maybe his work was too stressful, that he was just blowing off steam. But his words grew more and more hurtful, cutting her deeply. She'd lost weight before they were married, but eventually gained it back. He ripped on her because of her size. Toward the end he'd said to her that all of his friends had a hundred and twenty-five pound wives and all he had was a wife he considered to be too big.

Toward the end she hadn't known what to do. She'd considered leaving him, but she'd never lived on her own and didn't know if she could support herself with her home-based business.

And then it didn't matter. Bart had come home one night, told her he was leaving her for another woman, said a few more cruel things, packed his things and left.

Barb's not fat like you. The words still rang in her ears.

Even though she wanted children so badly it hurt, maybe it was better that she hadn't had any with Bart. There were no connections between them now and she could move on with her life, never having to deal with him again.

Except for his family. But that was okay. She wasn't going to let him end that relationship too.

The tears started to subside. She was over Bart. Some of the pain was still there, but he couldn't hurt her anymore.

Talking with Grace had affirmed that fact.

Megan took a deep breath and brushed away the remnants of tears with the backs of her hands.

"Stop it, Megan," she said out loud. "This isn't me."

She normally had a positive attitude, and she wasn't going to let him take that from her. She had a new life and potentially a great guy in Ryan. Who'd have thought?

It was more the sadness of what she considered a failure, even though she'd done everything she could to make their marriage work. The mistake had been thinking he could change.

She was resolved all the more to find someone who was different.

Life has a way of teaching lessons. Now she knew what to look for in a man and just maybe she had a good one now.

She sighed. Her concentration was shot. She might as well go look at the houses since she couldn't get her mind to focus on work. She'd just go ahead and work late into the night to make up for it.

Once again she thought about Ryan and the fact that he happened to be at a wedding himself. It could even be going on this very moment.

She groaned. *Stop obsessing over the man and go look at houses.* She picked up the cell phone and dialed the first number.

After making appointments with a realtor to take a look at some rental homes, Megan headed out of the house. She had some time before she met with the realtor, so she drove to the Hummingbird Café.

Her parents' café was quaint with an old-fashioned look to it. It was pretty with light blue trim on white and a blue and white striped awning. Flower boxes filled with geraniums were on the windowsill and a large hummingbird with flowers was painted on the front picture window. Three ironwork tables with matching chairs were on a patio in front of the restaurant for patrons to use when the weather was nice like it was now.

On the right side of the café was a convenience store and gas station which no doubt drew some patrons.

On the other side of her parents' place was an older restaurant with a sign that said *The Chuck Wagon* over the door. It had a western look to it with thick dark wood borders, and the place could do with a new paint job. She frowned. It had to be Roger Meyer's place.

People passed by on the street and a group stopped in front of the Chuck Wagon then went inside. A tall and lean man came out of that restaurant and started to walk past Megan toward the convenience store, but he stopped in front of her. He had brown hair and muddy brown eyes. He might have been considered good looking, yet his angular face seemed somehow at odds with his smile.

"You don't want to go in there." He jerked his thumb toward the Hummingbird Café. "Bad food and they've been in trouble with the Health Department."

Anger burned in Megan, making her face hot but she kept herself composed. "You must be Roger Meyer, the owner of the Chuck Wagon."

"Yes, I am." He grinned. "Best restaurant around."

"If your restaurant is so great," she said, "why do you have to tear down someone else's? Is your reputation not good enough to stand a little competition?"

Meyer's face darkened. "You must work for them."

"My parents own the Hummingbird Café." She stared him down. "Why don't you leave them alone and tend to your own business."

She didn't wait for a response and walked past him to the café. Skin on the back of her neck crawled as she could feel the jerk's eyes on her.

When Megan pushed open the door to the Hummingbird Café, bells danced in a playful jingle. She took a deep breath and then let it out, along with the heat of her anger.

The interior of the restaurant was cool and bright. The tables were set with white tablecloths and bud vases with single red carnations in each one. At night, the lights would be dimmed and tables set with a single votive candle for atmosphere. The chairs and tables were light blue to match the trim on the outside. Tables for two were along one side and the rest of the tables seated four but could be pulled together for larger parties.

It was closing in on noon, but only four of the tables were filled with customers.

A hostess station was at the front of the restaurant and Tess was standing beside it with an order pad in her hand.

"Hi, sweetie." Tess pushed a hand through her blonde waves. "Stop by for a bite to eat? Or for my great company?"

"Your great company, of course." Megan smiled. "Is Jenny feeling any better?"

Tess nodded. "She's with Mrs. Webb. That woman is incredible, especially to be watching her on a Sunday while I work."

"I'm glad Jenny is feeling better." Megan glanced over her shoulder and out through the large window to the street. She turned back to her sister. "I just met that Roger Meyer. What a jerk."

Tess frowned. "What did he do now?"

"Stopped me in the street and told me how bad this restaurant is and that I shouldn't come in here."

A look of irritation crossed over Tess's pretty features. "I wish that guy would just go away. I should put some roaches into the back of his kitchen and call the Health Department." She shook her head. "But I'd never stoop to his level."

Megan looked around the restaurant and said to her sister in a low voice, "Is it always this slow?"

"Ever since Roger started his vendetta against Mom and Dad." Tess scowled. "Of course it can't be proven that he was responsible, but we know he is."

"That sucks." Megan shook her head. "There's got to be a way to stop him and get traffic coming here."

"If you can think of a way, let us know," Tess said. "At this point we'd probably do anything to get customers coming in. I might start dancing in my panties and bra on the tabletops."

"Let's hope it doesn't come to that." Megan laughed. "Where are Mom and Dad? In the kitchen?"

Tess nodded. "Yep."

"I'll go say hello," Megan said.

Tess raised her order pad. "And I'd better get back to work."

Megan walked down an aisle between tables to the back and slipped into the kitchen. The busboy and dishwasher, Tucker, was busy washing and drying dishes. Paul was at the stove stirring a large pot of chili. Her father stopped stirring to taste the chili.

Margaret was rolling pie dough on a counter and flour was on her apron and on the tip of her nose. In front of her was a large bowl with peach slices glazed in sugar and next to that were two empty pie tins.

Megan breathed in the scent of peach pies baking in one of the ovens. "Making your awesome best in the west pies, I see."

Margaret raised her head. "Did you finish your work early?"

"I decided to go look at a few rental homes and find a month-to-month place until I figure out just where I want to live." Megan leaned up against a clean counter. "But I thought I'd stop by for a few moments and see how everything is going with you and Dad." She decided not to mention her brief conversation with Roger

Meyer.

Margaret placed the dough she'd just rolled into one of the pans for the bottom crust, then picked up another blob of dough and started rolling it out. "Better watch it or we'll put you to work."

"Except we all know that cooking, baking, and serving are not among my talents," Megan said. All things she absolutely hated. She'd helped her parents out with cleaning and washing dishes, but those tasks weren't among her favorite things to do by a long shot. She looked at her watch. "I've got to go meet with the realtor now."

Margaret rolled out the dough. "Anxious to move out?"

"Once I'm out you'll have your guestroom back," Megan said, wanting to avoid a guilt trip.

"You're welcome to stay as long as you like," Margaret said as she placed the raw crust into the second pie tin.

"I know, Mom." Megan gave her mother a smile. "It will be good for me to get my own place."

Margaret nodded. "Do what is best for you."

Megan tried not to sigh, but then realized her parents could probably use the regular income from the money she was paying them as rent.

She held back a groan. Was it her responsibility to stay with her parents and pay them rent instead of finding another house?

As much as she loved them, they drove her crazy. She wanted her own place with her own routine, and peace and quiet. She wanted to not have to worry about bothering anyone else, or anyone bothering her. Was that too much to ask for?

Well, she was still going to take a look at those homes and she'd think about staying with her parents to help them out a little longer. She didn't need to make that decision today.

Margaret's expression went hard as she looked past Megan. Paul stopped putting spices into the chili and he scowled. Megan glanced over her shoulder to see Roger Meyer standing in the doorway.

"Have a moment?" Meyer gave an amiable smile. "I'd like a few words with you both."

"We're busy." Margaret picked up a hand towel and started wiping flour off her hands. "We have a business to run."

Meyer looked over his shoulder into the dining room before turning his gaze back on Margaret. "Doesn't look so busy to me."

Paul narrowed his eyes. "We're finished here."

"I know you signed a lease." Meyer ignored Paul. "Your café is not doing well and you can't be making money. You have to be losing it."

Margaret gripped the hand towel and raised her chin. "Whether or not our business is profitable is no concern of yours."

"I'd be glad to take over your lease for you." Meyer kept the friendly smile on his face but there was a glint of something hard in his eyes. "You must be hurting for money."

"We're not interested." Growing anger was in Paul's voice.

Meyer frowned. "I'll give you five thousand in addition to taking over the lease. This offer is one time only. The moment I walk out that door, you can forget the five grand."

"No." The word came out of Paul in a short, sharp bark backed by anger. He raised the spoon he'd been stirring the chili with. "We have a business to run. See yourself out the front door."

"You'll regret this." Meyer gave a dark scowl as he turned around and strode out of the kitchen. A few moments later the front entrance bells jangled and the door slammed.

There was quiet for a minute in the kitchen then Paul returned to spicing up the chili and Margaret started rolling out another crust. Both looked angry, but neither said a word about what had transpired. Megan took their cue and didn't say anything about it.

"I'd better get going, Mom." Megan started backing up. She waved at Paul. "See you later, Dad."

His face still dark with anger, Paul gave her a nod then set down the chili spoon and began chopping vegetables on a cutting board next to the stove.

Megan turned and walked out of the kitchen, grinding her teeth at what had just transpired with Meyer. What an ass. Would he follow through and do something to hurt their business?

"What happened?" Tess came toward Megan in the dining room. "What was Meyer doing here?"

"He just offered to take over the lease and would give Mom and Dad five thousand if they accepted his offer today. Dad practically kicked the bastard out." Megan scowled as she looked at the entrance. "Meyer said they'd regret it."

Tess pushed her hand through her curls. "I wouldn't put anything past the man. According to Mr. Cowell, the owner of the building, Meyer threatened him when he was told Mr. Cowell wanted to sign a lease with us."

"You might not put anything past the man," Megan said, "but I'm not sure there's anything he can really do to the business. I think he's just a hateful man with a loud mouth."

Tess nodded. "You're probably right. It's just too bad we have such a jerk for a business neighbor."

CHAPTER 9

Ryan, as best man at his cousin's wedding, walked down the aisle beside Charity, the maid of honor, the ushers and bridesmaids in step behind them.

With her black hair and vivid blue eyes, Charity was downright gorgeous. But she knew it and flaunted it, which made her less attractive to Ryan. He preferred a woman like Megan who didn't realize how beautiful she was.

To either side of the procession the pews were filled on both the groom's and the bride's sides. Ryan and Charity reached the front of the church and took their places, followed by the four ushers and four bridesmaids. The men were in tuxes and the women were in dresses the color of Megan's glass-green eyes.

Tom, the groom, stood at his spot in front of the preacher

and looked toward the back of the church. The double doors were closed.

Ryan's thoughts turned to Megan and he mentally shook his head. He couldn't get the woman out of his thoughts. Not that he wanted to. He liked thinking about her and the next time they would be together, which would be when they went camping the following weekend.

His mind turned to thoughts of what they'd do. Fishing, swimming, and hiking. Maybe they'd even get to do a little snuggling near the fire.

The wedding march jerked him out of his daydream as the organist started playing it. Janie entered the church in a flowing white dress, her face covered by a veil. A pause seemed to fill the air and then someone sniffled.

Ryan watched Janie as she slowly walked to the front of the church in time with the march. For some crazy reason he pictured Megan behind the veil.

This time he almost let out a breath of frustration. His thoughts of Megan were bordering on obsession and were moving way too fast. That had never happened before—imagining that a woman he'd just met was walking down the aisle toward him. Hell, he'd never thought of any woman in that way.

Sure, he'd had a couple of serious relationships, but in the end they hadn't been serious enough. He damned sure hadn't started thinking of marriage.

And he'd only known Megan for all of two days.

Ryan continued to watch Janie as she reached the front of the church. Her father stepped beside her, took her arm in his, then presented her to Tom.

Janie's flowers trembled, showing how nervous she was, but the lacy veil was still over her face so Ryan couldn't see her eyes well.

The preacher spoke about God bringing the bride and groom together and how they stood in the presence of the Almighty to be joined together.

Tom and Janie exchanged vows and slid rings on each other's fingers and then the preacher pronounced them husband and wife. Tom lifted the veil, revealing Janie's radiant face before he kissed her.

Ryan smiled as his cousin and his new wife headed back down the aisle to start their new life together.

He wondered what it would be like to be married to someone that he cared about as much as Tom loved Janie.

And then he thought about Megan and wondered what she'd look like as a bride and what kind of wife she would be. She was sweet and fun, and seemed like the type of woman he could fall in love with.

He shook his head. It was much too soon to be thinking about love or weddings with a woman he'd just met.

Loud country music throbbed from the live band in the bar where the after-reception party was being held. The new husband and wife had taken off for their vacation in the Bahamas and it was time for the wedding party to party.

Ryan had changed into a western shirt, jeans, and a comfortable pair of boots, and had joined his buddies at the bar. He'd had enough of the tux and all of the formal picture taking and was glad to be able to relax. He leaned up against the bar next to one of the other ushers and knocked back a shot of whiskey before taking a swig of beer.

"How about a dance, cowboy?"

Ryan looked over his shoulder and saw Charity standing behind him, a look in her blue eyes that said "SEX" in capital letters. In the past he might have been intrigued, but not now, not after meeting Megan.

"Maybe another time," he said and gave her a nod.

"Come on." She put her glossy red lips into a pout. "What's one little dance going to hurt?"

Ryan left his beer on the bar with one of the guys who'd been in the wedding, then went with Charity to the dance floor. Unlike Megan, Charity was an expert at the two-step. He'd found Megan's attempts so damn cute, and by the end of the night she had been doing a fine job. Was it just two days ago that he'd danced with Megan?

Before he knew it, he found himself dancing a country waltz with Charity.

When the waltz was over, he excused himself, but Charity stayed at his side and slipped her hand into his. She stopped and pulled back, forcing him to stop.

"Come on, Ryan." She went up to him and hung on his arm. "I want to dance a little more."

"Not now." He removed her from his arm, took her by the shoulders, and set her apart from him. "I'm leaving."

"I'll go with you," she said. "I could use some air."

Ryan found his patience waning. "I'll see you around, Charity," he said as politely as possible. He turned and walked out of the bar, hoping she got the message.

To his relief, she didn't follow him and he walked the short distance to his hotel. He thought about how different Megan was from Charity. Megan was sweet and unassuming where Charity was forward and demanding.

When Ryan got to his room, he shut the door behind him then looked at the time on his phone. It was fairly early and since Arizona's time zone was behind Montana's, it shouldn't be too late to call Megan. He wanted to hear the sound of her voice.

From memory, he dialed her phone number.

She answered the phone on the third ring. "Hello?"

Smiling, he slipped off his western shirt, changing the phone from one hand to the other as he said, "Hi, Meg."

"Ryan?" She sounded surprised. "Hi."

"Thought I'd give you a call." He sat on the edge of the bed and started to toe off his boots. "How was your day?"

"Good," she said. "Busy." She paused. "I'm glad you called."

His boots thumped on the floor as he kicked them off. "Did you finish that website work that you'd planned to do this weekend?"

"I played a little hooky this afternoon and I'm trying to catch up tonight," she said. "I went house hunting for a place to rent."

He mounded the pillows against the headboard, sat on the bed, and rested against them. "Find anything you like?"

"A couple of places," she said. "I like one in particular because after ninety days the owner will let me go month to month until I can decide where I want to buy and how soon. I'll probably tell him I want it tomorrow morning before it's rented out from under me."

He shifted against the pillows "Where are you staying now?"

"With my parents," she said cautiously.

He stretched one leg out on the bed and bent the other knee. "I'd like to meet them sometime."

She hesitated and he wondered why. "Sure," she said and changed the subject. "How was the wedding?"

"The tux was a little tight around the collar." He rubbed his throat at the thought. "But the wedding was nice. Tom married a good woman and she got herself a good man."

Megan had a smile in her voice. "Sounds like a match made in heaven."

He nodded to himself. "I'd have to say it is."

"Speaking of weddings," she said. "My ex-mother-in-law called me to invite me to her daughter's wedding."

"You get along with your ex-in-laws?" He hadn't realized she was divorced.

"They're great," she said, but sounded a little sad, too. "They're the only part of my marriage that I miss."

He had the feeling she didn't want to talk about her marriage as she changed the subject again and asked about the reception.

"For a wedding reception it wasn't bad," he said. "A lot of our relatives were there so we did some catching up."

He told her a little more about it and about the party at the bar. Charity's persistence came to mind, but there was no reason to bring her up in any conversation he might have.

He asked her about the places she had checked out and what she was looking for in a house. She was practical and knew what she wanted. He liked that about her. She was also funny and cute and easy to talk with.

She yawned and immediately apologized. "That came out of

nowhere." She'd planned on doing website catch up but she didn't know if she could keep her eyes open.

"We'd both better get some sleep," he said. "Sweet dreams, Meg."

"Sweet dreams," she said softly before she disconnected the call.

CHAPTER 10

The following Friday morning, Megan picked up the duffel that she'd packed for the camping trip. It was 5:00 AM and she hoped neither of her parents was awake and she could leave a note on the fridge. She felt reluctant to tell them that she was going camping with a man she'd just met. All she needed was a grilling first thing in the morning like she was a teenager.

If she told her parents what she was doing, her mother would make some kind of remark about her not attracting the right kind of man because she wasn't the perfect size and her father would judge her for spending a weekend alone with a man she barely knew. She'd never hear the end of it. They would want to know his name and would probably check into him. She didn't need that.

She was a grown woman and she shouldn't feel like she'd be

punished or interrogated. She hadn't wanted her parents' negativity and hurtful remarks ringing in her ears as she walked out the door.

Now that she was back with her family, she wasn't so sure it had been the right step to take. But family was family.

Megan had moved to Prescott more to be with her sister and niece than for anyone else. Since she and Tess had always been close, it had been difficult once Tess and her daughter had moved away from Albuquerque to be with their parents.

As soon as Megan opened the door to her bedroom, the smell of coffee hit her. No such luck that neither of her parents were up. With her duffel over her shoulder, she headed into the kitchen.

"Hi, Mom," she said as she walked through the doorway.

Margaret turned from the fridge, a carton of eggs in her hand. "Good morning, Megan." She glanced at the duffel. "Where are you headed?"

Megan shrugged. "I'm going camping with a friend from Phoenix." It was mostly the truth, she just wasn't going to tell her mother that the friend was a man and the friend wasn't from Phoenix.

Margaret set the eggs on the counter and took a package of bacon out of the fridge. "Do I know your friend?"

"No." Megan felt antsy and barely kept from bouncing up and down on her toes. "I've got to go. I'll be home Sunday."

"You should give me your friend's name and number and where you're going." Margaret set the bacon package on the countertop. "In case of an emergency."

"I have my cell phone," Megan said. "But we might not get service in the mountains. We're going to Bear Canyon Lake."

Margaret frowned. "What if—"

"Everything will be fine, Mom. I've got to go." Megan turned and headed for the front door. She closed it behind her and took a deep breath then let it out in a rush.

When Megan was in her car, she pulled out the directions to Ryan's ranch that he'd emailed her and she had printed out. She smiled. He'd called almost every day this week while he'd been in Montana. He'd spent a few days with other friends while he was there and from what he'd told her, he'd had a good time.

The drive to his ranch didn't seem too far and she enjoyed the scenery as she drove through it. She exited the highway and traveled down a dirt road, passing an old barn and shed before she reached a ranch house at the end of the road.

The home looked to be about thirty-years-old and made of large brown blocks. The roof, eaves, sills, and doorframes were white and there was a rock path leading from the driveway to the sun porch. The front yard was desert landscaping and looked easy to keep up.

Out front was Ryan's silver truck with a new-looking cobalt blue camper trailer behind it. Ryan was loading fishing rods into the back. An Australian shepherd stood beside him, watching her drive into the yard.

An excited thrill went through her belly as Ryan turned and smiled at her. She parked and reached for her small purse. When she straightened, he was opening the car door for her. He took her hand and she climbed out. His old-fashioned gentlemanly manners were so sweet.

As soon as she was standing, he kissed her firmly then drew away and smiled. "It's good to see you, Meg." Most people called her by her full name, but she liked the way he called her Meg.

"It's good to see you, too." She smiled then looked at the black, grey, and white Australian shepherd. "What pretty blue eyes."

"This is Ossie." Ryan rubbed the dog beneath her chin. "She's the hardest worker on this ranch."

Megan held out her hand for Ossie to sniff. "She's beautiful."

Ryan patted Ossie's neck. "Don't let that go to your head, girl."

The dog looked at him and gave a short bark.

Megan heard the sound of sheep and cows. She looked toward one corral and saw about a dozen Suffolk sheep like the ones she had seen at the country fair. In a larger corral were some pure black Angus cattle.

"Next time you come I'll give you a tour of the place," Ryan said to Megan. "We'd better get going while it's still early. Ready to go?"

"I'm excited to go camping," she said. "I haven't gone since I was in an outdoor club in elementary school." She opened the trunk of her car. "I take it by the fishing rods that we're going fishing, too. I've never gone fishing."

"We'll go fishing at Bear Canyon Lake for rainbow trout." He took her duffel bag out of the trunk. "If you're half as fast at learning how to fish as you were learning how to two-step, you'll do just fine."

She closed the trunk. "Am I right that Bear Canyon Lake is on the Mogollon Rim?" She closed the trunk. "I looked it up on the Internet and saw that it's three and a half hours from here."

He nodded. "It's a bit of a drive but well worth it."

She smiled. "Can't wait."

"I just need to throw a few things into the ice chest and we're ready to go," he said as they started toward the house.

Ossie stayed close as they loaded the chest and packed ice around the sodas and beer along with sandwiches, condiments, butter, and a few other things that needed to stay cold. He also had bags with some canned items, aluminum foil, a can opener, marshmallows, crackers, an onion, potatoes, salt and pepper, snacks, and a few other items.

When everything was in the back of the camper, Ryan opened the passenger door of the truck for her and helped her inside.

He said goodbye to Ossie when he went around to his side. The dog trotted up to the house and onto the porch where she looked like she was standing guard.

"Will she be okay home alone while we're gone?" Megan asked as Ryan got behind the wheel.

"My ranch hands will make sure she's fed," he said. "She's a working dog, so she'll be helping them run the ranch while I'm away."

She suddenly felt tongue-tied. She was about to embark on a three-and-a-half hour drive with Ryan followed by a weekend together and then another long drive back. What if they ran out of things to say? What if he wasn't so crazy about her by the time the weekend was over?

She straightened in her seat forcing all negative thinking aside. She was going to enjoy herself and his company, and nothing was going to change that.

Just to ensure that nothing put a damper on her trip, she shut off her phone and stuffed it into her small purse and tucked it under the seat despite having told her mother she'd have the phone on. If anyone needed to get ahold of her, they'd just have to wait until she got back on Sunday. She doubted they could get cell service in the mountains, anyway.

"Do you go fishing often?" She studied Ryan's profile as they drove down the driveway. He was such a sexy cowboy with his rugged good looks and denim blue eyes.

He glanced from the road to her. "Did I tell you how cute you look this morning?"

Her cheeks warmed and she pulled at the hem of her blue T-shirt. "Thank you." She was simply wearing a T-shirt, jeans and sneakers, had her hair pulled back in a ponytail, and wore no makeup whatsoever.

"To answer your question, I go fishing or hunting every chance I get." He looked back at the dirt road and pulled up to a stop sign. "Which isn't often. Running a ranch keeps me busy."

"Who takes care of it all while you're gone?" she asked.

Ryan guided the truck onto the highway. "My part-time ranch hands put in extra hours when I'm not here and cover the weekend when they're normally off." He pressed the accelerator and the truck sped up. "In turn they get additional time off if they want to take it and I pay them a bonus." He glanced at her. "I'll introduce you when you take a tour of the place sometime."

"I'd enjoy that." Something about Ryan's company was calming and she relaxed in her seat. She hadn't realized she'd been so tense. He was so easygoing and she loved that about him.

They moved on to talking about Ryan's growing up around Prescott. Megan didn't really want to talk about her childhood so she kept turning the questions back to Ryan. He seemed to realize that she didn't want to discuss her past, and her divorce never came up. It wasn't something that was good fodder for a new relationship as far as she was concerned.

The drive went by faster than she expected. He told her the history of places they traveled through. Before they got up into high country, she admired the desert scenery. She loved the desert and how one could see for miles with nothing blocking the view.

On the way, they stopped at a small country store and Ryan paid for her fishing license as he already had one for himself. He also bought earthworms and Power Bait before they continued driving to their destination.

As they got into the mountains, he drove the truck into the forest and up a winding road. They traveled a while until they reached a side road that led to campsites he'd used before. The truck bounced along the dirt road, which was filled with potholes and rocks.

When they reached a good campsite in the midst of the forest, he backed the camper trailer into position. Once he'd parked the truck and camper, he climbed out, rounded the truck, and helped her out. He closed the door behind her as she stepped onto rich dark soil and she breathed in the amazing scent of the forest.

"Smells so wonderful." She took another deep breath and sighed in pleasure as she listened to forest sounds that included the buzz of bees near a patch of wildflowers, birds chirping and a squirrel chattering. "Sometimes the wind through the trees sounds to me like there's a river in the distance," she said.

Ryan paused and listened. "You're right. Never thought of it that way."

She looked around them. "I like this spot."

"I'm not much for improved campgrounds," he said. "I like Arizona where there is so much public land that it's easy to find a spot that's remote and set up camp there."

"That's great," she said. "What's first?"

"We make camp and have lunch." He went to the camper and disconnected the trailer from the truck. "Do you want lunch now or after we gather some firewood?"

"We might as well get anything done that needs to be taken care of and then we can relax," she said. "What's after lunch?"

"We go fishing."

"That will be fun." She moved closer to him. "What can I do?"

"Let's get firewood and set it several feet from the fire pit." He pointed to a large circle of stones made by previous campers. It was filled with ash and the remnants of wood that had been used for a fire. They gathered firewood of all sizes and stacked it off to the side to use later.

By the time they finished, it wasn't quite noon. They settled in camp chairs in front of the camper with the ice chest between them and ate roast beef and egg salad sandwiches and drank sodas.

The roast beef tasted wonderful, Megan thought, as she happily munched on her sandwich. It tasted even better than usual out here in the fresh air.

When they'd finished their sandwiches, he brought out a package of Oreo cookies and they both twisted theirs open and ate the frosting before finishing off the chocolate cookie.

"The right way to eat an Oreo," she said before licking the frosting off a second cookie.

She realized he was watching her with intensity in his gaze and her eyes met his. "I've never seen anyone look sexy while eating a cookie," he said with a grin.

Her face warmed. "Just wait until you see me eat marshmallows."

He laughed. "I'm looking forward to it."

CHAPTER 11

The September afternoon was cool and breezy as they prepared to head out to Bear Canyon Lake. They couldn't camp right on the lake but he said the spot he'd found was about three hundred yards from the water. They would hike down to it.

Before they left, Ryan loaded up a pack with some snacks, water and a blanket. He grabbed a float tube and tackle box out of the back of the camper and Megan carried the rods and the bag with earthworms and Power Bait in it.

The hike to the lake was nice and the breeze blew strands of hair around her face as she breathed in the scents of pine and fresh air. They walked down the incline through the forest on a well worn path and then suddenly they were out in the open with the lake stretched out before them.

The view was gorgeous with the lake surrounded by Ponderosa pine trees, and the stretch of shore they'd found was empty of other people. Small ripples disturbed the water that gently lapped at the rocky, muddy shore.

Her sneakers left imprints in the soft wet earth as they walked along the shore and she listened to the sound of an eagle screeching as it passed overhead.

When they reached a huge log near an outcropping of rocks, Ryan set the float tube and tackle box down and took the bag of bait and rods from her.

"There's nothing like a fresh fish dinner while camping," he said as he settled on the log.

"Yum," Megan said. "Sounds really good to me."

He motioned for her to sit beside him and she braced her palms to either side of her on the rough bark. She watched as he showed her how to tie sinkers and a hook on the fishing line and how to bait the hook by using one of the glowing pink balls of Power Bait.

"This bait and earthworms are best for trout for beginners," he said as he stood, holding the rod. "I'm going to show you how to cast your line."

She got to her feet beside him and paid attention as he instructed her. He cast the line first to show her how it was done. "Here. This is ten o'clock and two o'clock. You bring the rod back to ten o'clock and snap it forward to two o'clock."

The line glinted in the sunshine as the hook and sinkers dropped into the water a good distance offshore.

He then gave the rod to her and had her reel in the line. The mechanism made clicking sounds as she turned it. When the line was reeled in, he had her hold the rod as he guided her through the motions.

She laughed as she attempted to cast the line a third time. "Pitiful," she said as her hook and sinkers dropped into the water a few feet from shore.

"At least you made it in the water this time," he said in a teasing voice. "You're doing great. Try it again."

She went through the motions again but released too soon and her hook and line snagged in a nearby bush.

The line was hopelessly snarled in the bush so he cut the line along with the hook and sinkers. She wanted to attach the hook and sinkers herself so that she'd know how to do it the next time, so he guided her until she had them on correctly. Then she put some of the hot pink bait on her hook.

"Let's try it again." He coached her through the motions.

This time her hook and sinkers made it out into the water and she gave him a grin. "I did it."

"Here's how to hold it." He showed her what to do if a fish tugged on the line.

When she felt comfortable with it, she settled on the log as she held her rod

"Something's nibbling on our line." Ryan nodded to her rod almost at once.

She looked up to see the end bobbing up and down and she felt vibrations through the rod. The thrill of excitement tickled her skin. "What do I do?"

The rod started bouncing in earnest. "Looks like you've got him. Start reeling in your line. Not too fast, but steady."

Megan started turning the reel and felt the fish's struggle all the way to her fingertips. She saw a flash in the air above the water before it went below the surface again.

"I think you've got a good one," Ryan said. "Keep reeling him in."

Ryan helped her and the next thing she knew, a rainbow trout was flopping on the shore. "Great job, Meg," he said and she felt proud at catching her very first fish.

He showed her how to grab the fish and remove the hook from its mouth with a gloved hand. "I want to take a picture of you with your first fish." He smiled and took his phone out of the tackle box and the waterproof bag he'd put it in. "Now hold your fish by its jaw, like this."

She felt squeamish as she did as he demonstrated, but she wanted to prove to herself that she could do just about anything that he showed her.

He had her stand a few feet away from the shore in case she dropped the fish so that it wouldn't flop back in the water, then had her pose as he took the picture.

"Come on, sexy." He grinned at her. "Show me that trout."

Even though she hated having her picture taken, she laughed and struck a pose, holding the fish up like she was a model on the Price is Right, showing a contestant the next prize. After he took the picture, he showed it to her. It wasn't bad at all. Her smile was brilliant and she looked like she was having as much fun as she actually was.

She caught her breath as he gave her a firm kiss. He smiled, then helped her put the fish on a stringer. He'd staked the stinger to the shore and they put the fish in the water so that it would remain fresh.

"Go ahead and bait your hook and cast your line again." He sat next to her on the log. "Want to try an earthworm this time?"

She made a face but she said, "Okay... I'll try it." After all, she'd told herself she wasn't going to be squeamish.

He handed her an earthworm and told her how to put it on so that it would stay on.

"This is so gross," she said, but put the hook through the wriggling creature.

"Great job," he said. She looked at him and he planted a kiss on her lips. "Ready to cast your line?"

A thrill went through her belly from the feel of his lips against hers. She got to her feet and held the rod like he'd shown her earlier. "Ten o'clock to two o'clock," she murmured to herself and cast the line.

When it landed in the lake with a solid *plop*, she laughed and grinned at him. "I think I'm getting the hang of this."

He sat beside her again on the log and she watched him tie something little on his own line.

"What is that?" she asked.

"It's an artificial fly." He glanced up at her. "I'm going to do a little fly fishing from the float tube," he said. "We'll see what these guys prefer. An artificial fly, Power Bait, or an earthworm."

"Hopefully Power Bait is the most popular," she said. "I much prefer handling that over an earthworm."

She felt a hard tug on her line and swung her attention to it. "I think I've got another one."

He watched her rod bow and then it went straight then bowed again. "I think you do."

She stood, remembering what he'd told her to do, and reeled

in the fish. She bounced up on her toes as she grinned at him. "This is fun."

"You're a natural," he said.

He offered to help her, but she was determined to do everything on her own, no matter how icky it was. She grabbed the glove from the tackle box and removed the hook even as the fish nearly flopped out of her hand. She held on tightly as she put the fish on the stringer and let it wiggle out into the water on the end of the short links. She wasn't crazy about putting fish on a stringer because that meant putting the stringer's hook into the mouth of the fish and through its gill before clipping the end of the hook together.

"You've got this under control," he said, with obvious approval in his gaze. "I'm going to try a little fly fishing."

He waded out into the water with his float tube, carrying his rod. Over his shoulder, he said, "You can try the float tube if you'd like."

"I think I'm happy on the shore," she said with a laugh. "I'm afraid I'd fall right off trying to cast a line and maintain balance on that thing."

His float tube was a kind of large floating seat with places for his tackle and a stringer for any fish he might catch. He floated just offshore, close enough for them to easily talk with each other.

When he was positioned, he swung his rod but she couldn't see the line as it sailed out. He told her how to fly fish as he did it from the float tube.

They chatted as she caught her limit of four trout and he didn't manage to get anything. Her grin got bigger and he shook his head, smiling, and teased her with, "Beginner's luck."

It was late afternoon when he said, "Why don't we pack up and head on back to camp and fry up that trout?"

"Do I have to clean them, too?" she asked as they packed up, realizing that she *was* squeamish about that.

"I'll take care of cleaning them and I'll even fry them up." He rested his arm around her shoulder and kissed the top of her head. "You brought home the fish."

For some reason his saying "home" gave her a tingly feeling. It was silly, but something about it made her believe in possibilities…of things real and beautiful and that perhaps weren't too good to be true.

CHAPTER 12

When they returned to camp, Ryan built a fire and got a good blaze going. It was late in the afternoon, heading on toward evening. He set up a cleaning station behind the camper where he placed the cooler that they'd put the fish into to keep them fresh.

He picked up one of the fish. "Would you like to try your hand at cleaning the trout?"

Megan grimaced. "I'll let you do the honors." She paid attention as he showed her how to clean the fish. "That's definitely not something I'm crazy about doing," she said after he gutted the first one.

With a smile he said, "We can cook the fish with the head on or cut it off."

"I don't think I like the idea of something staring at me as I eat it." She made a face. "I vote for cutting off the heads."

He laughed. "You've got it." He put the cleaned fish in a bag in the cooler, just leaving the skin on and the bones in. They'd take the bones out after the fish were cooked. Once all four were cleaned, Ryan got out cornmeal, seasoning, a bowl, and a cast iron frying pan. He mixed the cornmeal and seasonings in the bowl then coated the trout with the mixture.

He fried the trout in a little shortening for a few minutes on each side using the frying pan on a grate over the fire. When the fish was ready, he put it on a tray and took out the bones and then handed her a plate and took one for himself. Megan took one and a half of the small fish while Ryan took two. They each put on their plates large spoonfuls of the potato salad that he'd packed in one of the coolers and spoonfuls of canned baked beans that had been heated up over the fire. Megan had sliced up part of an onion to go along with them.

He'd brought wine coolers for her and beer for himself since she'd told him that she didn't like beer the night they were at the restaurant.

"It's wonderful," she said after she savored her first bite of the delicious trout.

"Thanks to you," he said with a smile. "We'd have been eating hot dogs if you hadn't caught these."

She gave him a smile in return. "I had a great teacher."

As she ate, she found a couple of small soft bones they had missed in the trout and put them on her plate. She drank two wine coolers and was feeling very mellow while Ryan had a couple of beers.

The trout were small, but one and a half was enough to fill

her up. Ryan had the other two along with the half she'd left on the trout platter.

When they had finished eating and had cleaned up everything, it was still before dusk.

He gestured to the forest. "How about going on a short walk before it gets dark?"

"I would love that." She got up from the camping chair she'd been sitting in. "I'll get my jacket from the camper. Where's yours?"

He told her and she grabbed both jackets and they slipped them on. Before leaving camp he put out the fire and picked up his fly rod.

They walked toward a path they had noticed earlier on their hike back from the lake. The late afternoon was pleasant and the scenery was wonderful.

As they walked, she looked up at him and smiled. "Thank you for bringing me camping with you. This has been an amazing day."

He took her hand and squeezed it. "Thank you for coming with me. I've loved every minute of it." He gave her a quick kiss that made her smile even brighter.

Leaves, pine needles, and twigs crunched beneath their shoes as they made their way down a path that meandered through the woods. Birds twittered overhead and she heard the chatter of a squirrel. The air was cool and she was glad she had worn a jacket.

A good fifteen minutes from camp, he grasped her hand and brought her to a halt. He put his finger to his lips to tell her to be quiet, then gestured to their right. She squinted and tried to see what it was he was wanted her to see. Then she saw them—a pair of deer standing so still they almost blended with the forest. One of the deer looked majestic with its large set of antlers and Megan felt like the animal was staring right at her.

The deer stayed a few more moments then bolted into the forest. Three more deer she hadn't noticed before followed the first two, their black-tipped tails sticking up in the air.

"A herd. They were beautiful." Megan looked up at Ryan and smiled.

"Those were mule deer," he said. "You can tell the difference from whitetail deer by the configuration of their antlers and the black tips on their tails."

She tilted her head to the side. "Whitetail and mule deer grow antlers differently?"

"Yep." Ryan started moving and she fell into step beside him. "Mule deer antlers fork as they grow where whitetail deer antlers branch from a single main beam and curl in."

A woodpecker started drilling into a tree, the sound echoing through the forest. Megan looked ahead and saw a squirrel scamper up a tree and onto a branch.

When they reached the lake, Ryan nodded toward the water. "See the little trout rising?"

"Yes," she said as tiny ripples disturbed the water.

He stepped away from her, held out his rod, and cast it into the water. He slowly reeled in the line and almost immediately his rod bowed a little and then a shimmer rose in the air as he reeled in a small trout.

"That was fast," she said.

He unhooked the fish and tossed it back into the water, then cast his line again. He caught six trout in only about a dozen casts and released them all.

She shook her head. "You weren't trying earlier today, were

you," she stated.

He laughed. "This time of day and mornings are the best for fly fishing." He reeled in his line one more time and then they headed back toward camp.

It was nearly dusk by the time they got back. "I loved the walk and seeing the animals," she said. "Especially the deer."

He put up his rod and then said, "Since you like seeing game, how about some spotlighting?"

"I'm up for anything," she said. "What's spotlighting?"

"Come on." He jerked his thumb toward the truck. "I'll show you." He grabbed a spotlight from the camper and they both climbed into his truck that was disconnected from the camper.

"Along the back roads is best," he said as he plugged the spotlight into the cigarette lighter.

He started the truck, drove away from the campsite, and headed along a dirt road. He rolled down his window, and as he drove turned the spotlight on and held it up out of the window.

Intrigued, she watched as he angled the light so that it shone into the trees.

"Are those eyes?" she said with surprise as she looked into the forest. "They're everywhere."

"The spotlight lights up the animals' eyes." He slowed the truck. "Look there. A deer."

"That is awesome." She buzzed down the truck window as he continued on.

The air chilled her face as they drove along back roads, but she barely noticed as they saw more deer and numerous elk,

"That's a magnificent rack." Ryan gestured toward the elk when they spotted it.

Megan peered out at the creature. "By a rack do you mean the antlers?"

Ryan nodded.

"Is that where they get the term for a female?" she said as she turned to face him.

He grinned. "Yep."

She shook her head. "Men," she said but laughed.

"Well, hello there." Ryan gestured to the right and came to a stop. "A bear. And a pretty good sized one."

Megan's eyes widened as she saw the big black creature staring at them from about twenty feet away, and her heart rate picked up so that it throbbed against her chest. "I did tell you I'm scared of bears."

"We'll move on," Ryan said. "He won't bother us and we won't bother him."

"Sounds like a good idea to me." She looked from the beast to Ryan as he put the truck back into gear. "What about us sitting around a camp fire tonight with bears out there. I really didn't know there were going to be bears around."

"This is Bear Canyon." Ryan laughed, reached over, and pinched her chin. "But you don't need to worry about them. These are black bears and they don't want anything to do with us. In the last twenty years or so, despite millions and millions of people out camping in Arizona, there have been maybe a handful of bear incidents. People left out food or the bear was protecting a cub she felt was threatened. You have nothing to worry about."

Megan pouted her lower lip. "I don't want to be one of a handful of incidents. They scare me."

"Good thing you have me here with you, Megan," Ryan said

with a grin. "If one comes around, I will kick that bear's ass."

She held back a laugh. "You aren't stronger than a bear."

Ryan smiled raising an eyebrow. "You underestimate me. Actually I have a little assistance."

Ryan reached into the console of his truck and pulled out a holstered gun.

"Why do you have that with you?" Megan asked. "For those bears you said don't attack?"

"Naw. It's for you," he said. "To make you feel more at ease."

"If you are thinking about bears, you're having to keep one eye open looking for bears while you're kissing me. You aren't concentrating on me and it ruins the moment," she teased.

"Is that so?" He grinned. "It is all about me focusing on you."

"Well, I will admit the gun does make me feel a little safer." she said. "It was pretty cool getting to see a bear, though," she added. "As a matter of fact, it was great seeing all of the animals. Thanks for taking me."

He looked away from the road and met her gaze and smiled. "I liked taking you." He looked back at the road, found a place to turn his truck around, and they headed back to camp.

When they returned, Ryan built the fire up again. He turned on a camping lantern with LED lights and put it into the camper on low so that they'd have light later on.

"Do you like s'mores?"

"I've never had real s'mores on a camping trip," she said. "But I bet I'll love them."

"You're in for a special treat." He cut off two thin green branches from a tree and cleaned them so that he had two sticks. He sharpened the ends to points.

While he prepared the sticks, Megan got out the marshmallows, graham crackers, and a giant chocolate bar. On a small table near the chairs by the fire, Megan arranged the chocolate and graham crackers. He handed her a stick and she pierced a marshmallow with the sharp end and put a marshmallow on his stick, too.

As they stood beside the fire, shadows jumped and flickered around them, the light dim. The heat from the fire warmed her skin as they stood close to the fire pit, and they put their marshmallows on their sticks and into the flames.

The marshmallows bubbled, toasting immediately so that they were nearly black on the outside. He held both sticks as she took a graham cracker and piece of chocolate and put it beneath the marshmallow, then another graham cracker on top of it them, and pulled it all away from the stick. To start, they made one for each of them.

Ryan ate his in a couple of bites. When Megan bit into the treat, her eyes fluttered closed as she tasted the combination of flavors. She gave a small moan as she took another bite and opened her eyes. She finished the s'more and licked her fingers. "That was great."

"You did tell me to just wait until you ate a marshmallow." He looked at her with heat in his gaze. "I'd say that was worth the wait."

He stepped closer to her and brought his hand to her face. "You have a little chocolate, right here," he said and lowered his head. His tongue darted out at the corner of her mouth and then he was kissing her.

She tasted chocolate and marshmallows, and his masculine flavor all in one. She moaned again, this time from desire.

When he raised his head, he spoke close to her lips, his voice husky. "Ready for another one?"

"Another kiss? Most definitely." She knew that wasn't what he'd meant, but she smiled and kissed him.

This time he groaned. He settled his hands at her waist and drew her closer to him so that their bodies were pressed together. Her belly fluttered as she felt the firm ridge of his erection against her abdomen. She wrapped her arms around his neck and his chest was hard against her breasts.

Their kiss grew almost frantic. She wanted to rip his clothes from his body, take him to the ground, and ride him. She didn't care that they were in the middle of the forest. All she cared about was being with him.

He was the first to draw away. "Whoa." He stepped away from her and caught her wrists in his hands. "I think we've got a runaway horse here. If we keep this up, I'm going to be carrying you to that camper and to hell with separate bunks."

Yeah, to hell with that.

She was going to say so when he released her and turned back to the table with the s'mores ingredients. His jaw was tense and there was a fire in his eyes that seemed barely controlled.

He grabbed one of the sticks and jammed a marshmallow on it. She could see the play of muscles in his forearms as he moved.

She went to him, caught his face in her hands, and kissed him.

"Meg, my self-control is on a thin leash." His breathing seemed heavier and the flash in his eyes was like a flame licking in their depths. "You don't know what you're doing."

"I know exactly what I'm doing." She brought her mouth to his and kissed him hard.

He dropped the stick. And then his arms were around her and he was kissing her with fierce intensity, like he might come undone.

She wanted him to come undone. Wanted him in every way possible.

He grasped her by her ass and picked her up, and she wrapped her thighs around his hips. He stopped kissing her long enough to walk to the camper and fling open the door. Their eyes met and held for a long moment.

"Are you sure, Meg?" His voice was low and gravelly.

She nodded. "Very."

He set her down long enough to turn around and kick dirt on the fire, then grasped her hand.

And then they were taking the three steps up into the camper and he shut the door behind them.

CHAPTER 13

Ryan pressed Megan close to his body. He was hard, lean, and muscular and his cock felt rigid against her belly. Butterflies swooped through her abdomen as she looked into his eyes and the burning depths of desire that was just for her.

She'd never really thought of herself as desirable, but he made her feel gorgeous and sexy, and completely wanton.

The light from the lantern was low and part of her was glad it was on so that she could see his gorgeous eyes and his rugged features. The other part wanted darkness because she was self-conscious about her body.

He kissed her, sliding his fingers into her hair before moving his palms down her neck to her shoulders. He rubbed her shoulders and her arms, caressing her through her T-shirt. His kiss was hungry and demanding, and she felt like he could lose control at any moment.

She wanted him to lose control.

"I love your curves." He moved his hands down her sides, along the indentation of her waist and over her jeans to her hips. He grabbed her ass and squeezed the globes. "Your ass is so sexy."

He slid his hands back up to her T-shirt and grasped the hem. Her heart beat faster and she gave a hungry moan as he started to push the shirt up and over her breasts. He raised his head, breaking the kiss.

She helped him pull the T-shirt over her head, leaving her in her bra with the cool air brushing her skin. He tossed the shirt on the table behind him then cupped her breasts, almost reverently. "I love these. They fill my hands."

Heat flushed through her body, her excitement rising as he told her how much he loved her attributes.

He reached up and pulled her hair out of its ponytail and let it fall around her shoulders. His carnal expression sent thrills through her as he slid his hands into her hair and rubbed her scalp with his fingertips.

"Damn you're beautiful, Megan. Every part of you." He searched her gaze with his. "From the first moment I saw you I knew that I had to get your attention and get to know you better."

"I'm glad you did." Her voice was low. "I like you a lot, Ryan."

I'm really starting to care for you, too, she thought. The kind of caring that was dangerous to her heart.

He wrapped one finger in her hair then let his hand slide down to her shoulder. He moved both hands to her breasts again and she caught her breath as he pinched her nipples through her bra. She put her hands over his as he squeezed her breasts and their gazes met and held.

"Don't stop." Her throat was dry as she said the words.

He moved his hands up to her bra straps and drew them down, over her shoulders. "The only way I'm stopping is if you tell me to."

"I'm not going to," she said. "I wouldn't be here if I didn't want you so much that I can hardly bear it."

"I'm glad you're here with me. I've wanted you all day long, but I didn't want to take advantage of you." He kissed her bare shoulder, his mouth whisper soft against her skin. "You're the most sensual woman I've met. Everything about you is sensual."

His words sent wild sensations spiraling through her. She'd never thought of herself as sensual, but the way he said it made her believe that he meant it.

She tilted her head back as his lips trailed to the hollow of her throat and he flicked his tongue out to taste her salty flesh. He slid his hands from her shoulders and moved them around her and when his fingers reached her bra clasp he deftly unfastened it and tossed her bra aside.

It surprised her that she didn't feel self-conscious with him anymore. He made her feel beautiful and wanted.

He cupped her large breasts in his hands. "Gorgeous," he murmured before lowering his head and licking a nipple.

She gasped as he slipped the nipple into his mouth and sucked it. He flicked his tongue across it and she moaned with pleasure. His fingers pinched and pulled her opposite nipple and the sensation of his mouth and hands on her heightened her arousal. He kissed a moist trail to the valley between her breasts then licked her other nipple and sucked.

The light was behind him and it cast light on her but his face was shadowed as he raised his head. He kissed her again and she found she was having a hard time catching her breath as he brought her up hard against him again, her bare breasts pressed into his T-shirt and muscled chest.

He studied her face. "I like it hard and rough, Meg. Can you handle that?"

Her belly flip-flopped at the rough sound and intention in his voice.

"I can handle anything you give to me," she said. "Anything you want from me."

"I want it all," he said before he gave her a fierce kiss. He moved his hands to the button of her jeans and unfastened them before pulling her zipper down. "Sit on the bunk," he said and guided her back. She sat on the blanket-covered bed that was almost full-sized.

He grasped one of her shoes and she braced her hands on the bed to either side of her as she watched him remove her shoe. He peeled off her sock then picked up her other foot and removed the shoe and sock from it. Her feet were bare and all that was left were her jeans and panties. The moment seemed almost unreal as he started to strip her clothes from her body.

"I can't help but want to see you naked." He gently pushed her so that she was now on her back. "I want to look at your beautiful body."

For a moment she felt that old raw embarrassment from years of thinking that she wasn't good enough. But those thoughts fled as she met his gaze and saw not only the heat of desire and a look of reverence, but caring, too.

He grasped the waistband of her jeans and tugged them down, and she raised her hips to make it easier for him. He revealed her silky black panties as he pulled the jeans all the way off then let them drop to the floor. She was left in only her panties. Her heart beat faster as he slid those off of her, too.

He put his knee between her thighs, parting them wide as he stepped between them. He studied her as she lay naked on the bunk, spread out before him, and his eyes smoldered with desire. She bit her lower lip as she looked up at him, wanting him so badly that she could barely lie still.

The rough material of his jeans brushed the insides of her thighs as he lowered himself so that he could brace himself over her, his hands to either side of her shoulders. He kissed her hard, his lips taking control of hers as he slipped his tongue into her mouth.

When her head was spinning from his kiss, he rose up and took her hands in his and brought her up to stand with him. He brought her naked body tight against his, his T-shirt rubbing her nipples and his jeans abrading her soft skin.

His hands slipped into her hair and grasped a handful, then pulled her head back, catching her off guard. "I told you I like it hard and rough." His gaze held hers. "Are you sure you can handle me?"

"Yes," she whispered.

"Louder, Megan," he said. "I want to hear you say it."

"I want it rough and hard." She swallowed. "I can handle anything."

His stare was primal, almost wild. With her head still pulled back, he kissed her throat, biting her with small nips of his teeth and tongue. She clung to his biceps as his mouth reached her nipple and then she cried out when he lightly bit it.

He released her hair as he stepped back and pulled his T-shirt over his head and ditched it. He took her into his arms and her nipples brushed his bare chest as he moved her around so that he could sit on the bunk and take off his boots and socks.

"I want you to play with your breasts." His words were a demand.

Embarrassment flooded her. She'd never touched herself in front of a man.

"Come on, Megan." One of his boots thumped on the camper floor as he let it drop.

She raised her hands and brought them to her breasts and pushed them together so that her cleavage was deep and her nipples jutted out. She rolled her nipples between her fingers and was surprised at how erotic it felt playing with herself with a man watching. With Ryan watching.

"That's it," he murmured as he let his other boot drop to the floor. "Now touch yourself between your thighs."

Heat flushed through her and she hesitated again.

"You said you could do anything I wanted of you," he said. "I want to see you do it."

She bit the inside of her lip as she slowly let one of her hands slide from her breast, down her belly to the juncture of her thighs. He gave a nod as she watched him and she slipped her finger into her wet folds.

As she moved her finger over her clit, she felt unbelievably aroused. There was something about doing this with a man she cared about, who she was sure cared about her.

"Keep playing with your nipple, too." His voice was rough as he stood and unfastened his belt buckle while he watched her. He pulled his belt out of its loops and held the long strap in both hands.

Her knees felt almost weak from need as she slid her fingers in and out of her folds and played with her nipple as he watched. He stepped forward and looped the belt around her shoulders, catching her off guard as he pinned her arms to her sides and jerked her to him.

With her arms pinned, she couldn't touch herself anymore. He had her in his control. He moved his hand down and slid his fingers into her folds and this time her knees almost gave out.

"Nice," he murmured. "You're so wet. I could slide into you right now and take you 'til you scream. Is that what you want?"

She swallowed and nodded as his touch brought her closer to orgasm.

"Say it." He moved his lips to her ear. "Tell me exactly what you want."

"I want you to take me." The words came out soft at first, but then she spoke a little louder. "I want you to take me hard."

His smile was so carnal, so heated, that she found herself coming closer to orgasm as he rubbed her clit.

"Do you want to come?" he asked as he watched her.

She stared into his eyes. "Yes."

"You're going to have to wait. I'm not going to let you come yet." He slipped his fingers out of her folds and she gasped at the sudden loss of contact.

He cupped the side of her face and kissed her. She moaned

as he devoured her lips and made her feel like he was showing her how much he cared. Tender yet insistent.

When he took a step back, he moved his belt from her shoulders and fastened it around her at her waist and elbows. Then he watched her as he unbuttoned his jeans and pushed them over his hips along with his boxer briefs, then kicked them aside.

His body was magnificent, power evident in his corded muscles. They were well defined, tense, and his jaw was tight as he clenched his hands at his sides like he was going to lose control. A light sprinkling of hair was on his chest and his features were dark and intense.

She looked at the length and girth of his cock—he was so big. She ached between her thighs at the thought of having him inside her.

He stepped closer and took her by her shoulders. "On your knees," he said, the power in his voice sending a shiver down her spine.

With her elbows pinned to her waist she felt off balance as she started to kneel, but he steadied her as he continued to hold her by the shoulders while she went down.

When she was on her knees, his cock was before her face. She tilted her head back and looked into his eyes, feeling as if she needed to wait for his next instructions.

"Suck my cock." He pressed his erection against her lips. "I know you want to."

"Yes," she said and he pushed his cock into her mouth.

He grabbed a handful of her hair and pulled her hair back again. "I want to see your eyes as you go down on me."

His control excited her in ways she had never imagined.

She took him deep as he guided her with his hand on the back of her head, and she was still unable to move her arms. He tasted salty and good and she loved the way he watched her with fierce intensity.

He might like being rough and dominant during sex, but she could tell that there was more to it with him. Sex wasn't just sex between them. She felt it with everything she had.

"That feels so damn good." Then his expression grew almost pained as his jaw tensed and he gritted his teeth. He pulled her head back farther and drew his cock out of her mouth. "I don't want to come yet. I want to take you hard."

"Yes," she whispered as she looked up at him.

He released her hair and caressed the back of her head then took her by the shoulders. "I want you to stand." When she was on her feet, he kissed her. "That was so hot," he murmured as he drew away. "Watching my cock going in and out of your mouth."

She licked her lips. "I loved it."

He unfastened the belt from around her arms and waist. "Sit on the edge of the bunk then lie on your back."

She obeyed and he knelt between her knees, pushing them apart with his big shoulders. She tingled between her thighs as his naked body pressed against her bare skin and she ached for his touch.

As she watched him, he slid two fingers into her core and her eyes widened as she arched into his touch. He started moving his fingers in and out, down to his knuckles. With his eyes fixed on hers, he lowered his head and licked her folds in one long swipe.

Her cry was almost a shout from the sensations that hit her hard. As he licked and sucked her clit he reached up and palmed her breasts and played with her nipples.

Fire seared her as she began approaching orgasm at once. She came closer and closer to the peak, light growing brighter in her mind.

"That's it," he murmured as he raised his head. "I want you to come."

He made a rumbling sound as he put his mouth back on her and sucked her clit.

She came so hard her hips bucked against his face. Every sensation, every thought spiraled in her mind as her body shuddered from the power of her climax. He continued to lick her until she couldn't take anymore.

Her body was still throbbing as he rolled her onto her belly. "On your knees."

She started to get on all fours but he braced his hand on the back of her head and held her down in a dominant hold so that she was on her knees, her face against the blanket, her forearms on the bed. He was still standing, the bunk at the perfect height to take her from behind.

He released her head and she heard the sound of a foil packet tearing. Her heartbeat sounded louder in her ears as she felt his cock pressing against the entrance to her core.

She started to raise her head to get on her hands and knees and rock back, but he put his hand on her neck, holding her down as he grasped her hip with his other hand.

He drove in hard and fast. She cried out from the sudden fullness and the depth that he reached. He started thrusting in and out and she moaned from the incredible feel of his cock inside her. His hips slammed against her ass and his hand gripped her tight.

"Do you like that, baby?" He continued taking her hard. "Do you like it rough?"

"Yes," she gasped. "*Yes.*"

He drew his cock out of her. "On your back now."

She obeyed and looked into his eyes and saw the wild light there that made the flutters in her belly even more frantic. He drew her legs around his waist as he pressed between her thighs. She crossed her ankles behind him as he drove in and out of her so hard her breasts bounced with every thrust.

He leaned over her and grasped her large breasts in his hands and pinched her nipples as he took her. She loved the feeling of him inside her, loved the way he looked at her. More than lust was in his eyes…a deep intense look of caring was there, too. He might like it hard and rough, but he also shared a connection with her that was almost tangible.

A climax came rushing toward her as their gazes held, and then she came with a cry that had to have echoed through the forest. The look in his eyes made the orgasm even stronger and it seemed to carry on longer than she ever remembered happening before. It was the most amazing orgasm she'd ever felt.

She watched as his jaw tensed and the look in his eyes somehow grew darker than before.

He came with a growl, a rumbling sound that sent vibrations through her. He moved in and out of her as he stretched out her orgasm along with his. She thought that neither of their orgasms would ever end. They seemed to last forever.

And then he drew out of her and braced his arms to either side of her chest, breathing hard with sweat rolling down his forehead. He looked at her a long moment then lowered his mouth to hers and kissed her softly.

He adjusted her on the bed so that he could lie down beside her. When he was settled, he propped himself up on his elbow and forearm as she rested on her back. He looked down at her and smiled as he brushed her hair from her face.

"Was I too rough?" he asked. "I couldn't control myself with you."

"You weren't too rough." She smiled. "I loved every moment."

He lowered his head and brushed his lips over hers. "I love the woman you are. I love everything about you."

She swallowed as she looked up at him to read the meaning in his eyes. He appeared so focused on her that he might be unaware of everything around him but her. Caring was there, the same caring she'd seen all day. He hadn't hidden it from her and she didn't think she was reading him wrong.

Just how much he cared for her, she didn't know, but it was there.

She reached up and touched the side of his face. "I feel the same way you do."

He smiled and lowered his head and kissed her again. When he drew away he reached for a blanket at the foot of the bed and pulled it over them before settling himself so that he could bring her into his arms, her head resting on his chest.

A loud crash startled Megan awake.

The sound came from outside the camper. Ryan was already out of bed and putting on his clothes.

Her heart pounded as she sat in bed holding the blanket to her naked breasts. "What is it?"

He looked out the window. "A bear. Looks like he got ahold of the trash."

She put her hand over her mouth before she lowered her hand and said, "I forgot to seal it and put it in the back of the truck."

Another crash caused her to jump.

"It's tearing up camp." Ryan reached into the drawer beside the bunk and drew out his pistol. "I'll scare it off."

Her eyes widened. "Are you sure? Are you going to shoot it?"

"Bears are scared of humans." He reached for the door handle. "No, I don't plan on shooting it. This is just to help scare it off."

A third crash and Ryan jerked open the door, swept his gaze over the scene, and shouted, "Get out of here," in a loud, powerful voice.

Megan scrambled into her T-shirt and jeans as she peered out the door and watched Ryan make a bunch of noise and holler. The creature gave a guttural cry then turned and lumbered into the forest.

Heart pounding, Megan stood in the doorway and stared in the direction the bear had disappeared. "Will it come back?"

"Not likely." Ryan shook his head. "But let's clean up the trash to avoid anymore nighttime visitors."

"Oops." Sheepishly, she looked at him. "I'm the one who's afraid of bears and I led one right to us."

He laughed. "I think it wasn't just the trash. We forgot about those left over s'mores."

She couldn't help but keep looking over her shoulder, wondering if the bear would show up again, as she helped Ryan gather all of the trash scattered across the campsite and seal it all in a new bag. They also righted the camping table and chairs.

When they were finished, he put the sealed bag in the back of the truck where a bear couldn't climb then put his arm around her shoulders and walked to the camper. He let her head up first and then he closed the door and locked it behind them.

She slid out of her clothes again and climbed into bed and into his arms. His warm, naked body heated hers through.

It wasn't long until she slipped back into dreamland, Ryan's powerful embrace chasing her fears away.

CHAPTER 14

Megan woke to sunshine and the feel of a warm naked body next to hers. She opened her eyes and saw Ryan watching her.

He skimmed a finger along her arm. "Good morning, beautiful."

She smiled at him. "It certainly is a good morning."

He trailed his finger up one breast to her nipple. "Are you ready for breakfast?"

"Yes." She placed her hand on his hard chest. "But if you keep that up I might not let you out of bed."

His smile was entirely sexual. "Don't tempt me."

"Hmmm…" She played with his flat nipple. "Let me think about that."

The flare in his eyes was unmistakable. He rolled her onto her back and moved between her thighs, causing her belly to swoop. He reached into the drawer near the head of the bunk and pulled out a foil packet. He tore it open with his teeth then sheathed his cock.

She didn't realize she'd been holding her breath until he slid inside her and she let out his name on a gasp of pleasure.

He moved in and out of her, his gaze focused on hers. His stokes were smooth and slow as he watched her. The way he looked at her made her feel like she really was beautiful.

An orgasm started to build inside her and her mind started to whirl. When she saw the tenseness in his jaw, she knew he was close to coming, too.

Her back arched as her climax tore through her and she cried out. Her thoughts whirled and she was barely conscious of Ryan. But she felt his body cord and then he was groaning as his cock throbbed inside her.

He hugged her then braced his arms and looked down at her. "That was a fantastic way to start out the morning."

She smiled. "Incredibly amazing."

He eased off of her and slid off the bunk, then ditched the condom in a small trashcan. He held out his hand. "Ready to get up?"

She took it. "Can't wait to see what you have planned for the rest of today."

First thing, Ryan built a fire and heated some water to wash up. Megan washed her face and sponged off then dressed in a T-shirt, shorts, and sturdy athletic shoes. She pulled her hair back into a ponytail.

When she came out of the camper, she smelled bacon at once

and saw a platter of bacon nearby, along with hash browns. He was frying eggs in the cast iron pan on the grate.

She held her hand to her belly that growled instantly. "That smells wonderful." She reached the fire pit and felt heat on her skin. "I'll get the plates and forks."

He smiled gestured toward the camping table. "Everything is over there."

She grabbed what they needed, including a couple of paper towels. They ate everything he'd made.

"Breakfast was incredible," she said and reached for his empty plate.

He handed it to her, and she took everything and put it into the garbage bag by the camping table while he cleaned up wrappers and the frying pan.

"Are you up for a hike?" He gestured in the opposite direction of the lake. "We can drive in over there and go up to one of the fire towers."

"I'd love to," she said.

They put out the campfire and made sure the garbage and food was in the camper, then drove a good distance into the forest. After he parked, they started hiking up the mountainside. Through the trees she could see the tower that was a good distance above them.

As they hiked, Ryan pointed out different plants and named the varieties, and he was familiar with a lot of the bird species, too. By the time they reached the fire tower, she was out of breath, but she felt fantastic. The clean, fresh scent of the cool air was invigorating and the hike with Ryan had been exhilarating.

She looked out at the forest spread out below them. "The view is incredible."

"Let's see if the spotter is here and maybe he'll let us climb up into the tower," Ryan said.

She looked dubiously at the tower. "That looks really high. I think I might suddenly be afraid of heights."

He grinned. "It's worth it."

Ryan climbed up the tower and a panel in the floor opened. She saw him talking to someone but couldn't hear what he was saying.

He looked down and waved to her. "Come on up."

She bit her lip but went to the tower. She put her hands and one foot on the metal rungs and looked up.

He gestured for her to follow him up. "You can do it."

She took a deep breath and started to climb, but wouldn't let herself look anywhere but up at Ryan.

When she reached the open panel in the floor, he helped her climb the rest of the way inside.

"Welcome," a man said as he extended his hand. "I'm Don." He had gray hair, tanned skin, and wore a bright red shirt that had "U.S. Forest Service FIRE" on the front on the upper left hand side.

"I'm Megan," she said then caught her breath the moment she looked from the man and out of the windows at the 360-degree view. Miles of forest spread out before her with majestic mountains in the distance. She could see a large lake and acres of green grasses in the midst of the forestlands.

"Wow." She stepped away from the man to the lookout windows. "This is incredible."

"Worth the climb?" Ryan asked.

"I'll tell you as soon as my feet are safely back on the ground."

She smiled at him. "But yes, it's pretty incredible."

The spotter showed them points of interest and Megan couldn't get over all that they could see from their vantage point. Don let her look through his field glasses, but most of the time he continued to look around the forest to watch for fires.

"The fire season is ending in a week," Ryan said. "They close up the fire towers depending on the conditions. Usually they close them when the rains come in the fall and then they generally won't open them again until May."

"I'm glad we had the chance to see the view from up here," Megan said.

"Why don't we head on back to camp?" Ryan said.

Megan looked out one last time then turned to the spotter. "Thanks for letting us come into the lookout."

"It was nice having a little company," Don said.

Ryan went down the ladder first then Megan followed. She refused to look at anything but the ladder as she climbed down, doing her best not to look at the ground or at the forest stretched out before them.

She gave a huge sigh of relief when her feet touched the ground and Ryan steadied her. He gave her a kiss. "I hope you enjoyed that."

"Immensely," she said then added, "Minus the climb," and he tugged her ponytail.

The way back down the trail was easier because it was downhill and it didn't take them too long to reach the truck.

It was noon by the time they reached the campsite and they had the rest of the sandwiches from the cooler along with barbeque chips and cream soda. She hadn't had cream soda since she was a kid.

"How about a little skinny dipping in the lake?" he asked when they finished eating.

She raised her eyebrows. "What if someone comes?"

He grinned "The danger makes it all the more fun."

She laughed. "I could use a little danger in my life."

This time they didn't bring any fishing tackle when they walked to the lake, but they did take a couple of towels.

She glanced at him as they walked and smiled to herself. Ryan was a man's man but he was so energetic and liked to have fun. She loved being with him, loved everything about him.

With Ryan she felt safe...protected...cared for...maybe even more.

She'd never had this feeling with her ex—all he'd ever done was go to the office and come home and sit his butt in front of the TV and watch sports or play golf with his friends.

Why hadn't a guy like Ryan been snapped right up by some beautiful woman?

When they reached the lake, they stripped out of their clothing and put it all on a large boulder with the towels. Normally she would feel shy or embarrassed undressing in front of anyone, much less a man. For some reason she was okay with Ryan watching her strip. Maybe it was the appreciation in his gaze or the fact that he told her he could barely keep his hands off of her as she undressed.

The early afternoon sun was warm on her skin, but the breeze was cool. "The water's cold." She shivered despite the warmth of the sun as she stepped into the water along the rocky shore.

But even as she shivered, she had to admire his incredible body. She wanted to run her palms over his chest and feel his narrow hips between her thighs again.

"It's only a little cold." He stepped into the water, took her hand, and led her into water up to her knees, right before a fairly deep drop-off. "It's been a particularly warm September so the water isn't too cold, it's refreshing. Let's dive in."

"Refreshing? You're crazy." She shook her head but smiled at his boyish enthusiasm. "I think this is far enough. I'm going to go right back and get back into my warm clothes again."

"It's best to just take the plunge," he said with a devious grin as he grasped her around the waist.

"Oh, no." She shook her head and grabbed his shoulders. "Don't—"

She cried out as he picked her up and tossed her into the lake. She went down below the surface and came up sputtering and wiping water from her eyes. "That wasn't fair," she said but couldn't stop laughing.

He dove in and came up beside her. He brought her close and cut off her laughter with a soul-searing kiss. They pressed their wet naked bodies together and his skin felt slick against hers. The heat of his kiss matched the warmth of the sun beating down on them and she felt some of the cold dissipate.

When he drew away, he said, "Forgive me for tossing you in?"

She smiled. "Only if you kiss me again."

He caught her face in his hands and brought his mouth to hers. She slipped her hands around his neck and slid her fingers into his wet hair, her bare breasts rubbing against his chest as she hooked her legs around his hips. Despite the cool water she felt the heat of his body and the heat of his kiss warming her through.

When he broke the kiss, he didn't let go. He looked down at

her, a smile tipping the corners of his mouth. "I might be falling for you, Meg."

Her eyes widened and her lips parted. She was too surprised to find words.

Ryan, falling for her? She wasn't sure how she felt, but she was pretty sure she was falling for him, too.

Her throat worked. Before she could say anything, he gave her a firm kiss. "Come on. Let's swim."

His words kept going through her mind as they swam and played in the water. Just as they were about to go back, Ryan said, "I hear voices."

"Oh, no." She lowered herself in the water so that she was submerged from the neck down.

A couple walked out of the trees and down a path a little ways away, fishing poles in their hands. The man and woman waved and Ryan waved back. Megan was too afraid she might reveal something she didn't intend to if she waved.

The pair walked closer. Ryan glanced at Megan then at the couple again. "Would you mind turning the other way? We need to get to our clothes."

The woman laughed and the man said with a big grin, "Go right ahead. We like to watch."

Megan's eyes widened as she and Ryan looked at each other.

"We'd rather not," Ryan said.

"My husband is just teasing." The woman shook her head. "Come on, Garth. Let them have some privacy."

Still chuckling, the couple turned away and busied themselves with their tackle. Megan and Ryan hurried out of the water to the towels and their clothes. Megan hurried to wrap herself in a warm towel and dried herself off without revealing too much.

While holding the towel she managed to get her T-shirt and shorts on and just shoved her panties and bra into her pocket.

The man and woman kept busy until Ryan told them they were dressed. When the pair turned around, Megan was still putting on her socks and shoes. Ryan picked up the wet towels and put them under his arm.

"Have a good one," the man said to them with a grin.

"We plan to." Ryan winked at Megan. Looking back to the couple, Ryan said, "Good luck fishing."

The couple prepared to cast their lines as Ryan put his hand on Megan's shoulder as they walked into the forest and headed back to the camp.

CHAPTER 15

Ryan smiled as he walked back to the campsite with his hand on Megan's shoulder. He loved the feel of her soft skin and having her close to him.

No matter what he'd suggested she'd been game for it all. She'd even handled the fish by herself. Women he'd been around in the past had been too squeamish to bait a hook with an earthworm much less handle a fish.

She was beautiful and fun and everything he'd ever wanted in a woman.

He wasn't about to let her get away from him.

When they returned to camp, they changed into dry T-shirts and jeans and hung their wet clothes on a branch to dry.

"Ever play washers?" he asked after Megan finished combing

through her wet hair.

She shook her head. "I don't think so."

"I'll teach you." He brought out two short pipes that were four inches long and four inches in diameter. He had two sets of two and a half inch metal washers with a one-inch hole in the middle. "Red or blue?" he asked.

"Red," she said and he handed her the three red washers while he kept the blue.

"There are only two of us, so we'll use one pipe." He set aside the second pipe. "Getting your washer inside the pipe wins three points," he said. "The other washers receive points based on prox-imity. A point per washer for every one closer than the opponent's closest washer. Just like horseshoes."

She nodded. "I have played horseshoes, so I've got it. In fact, I hope you're a good loser, Ryan. I can really play horseshoes."

With a grin he said, "Oh, is that so?"

She matched his grin. "Just watch me."

He dug a hole, put the pipe in the ground, and softened and smoothed the ground around the pipe. When he finished they stood twenty-five feet from the pipe. "Toss them like this," he said, and threw his washers. Both landed close to the pipe.

It was similar to horseshoes and she caught onto the game fairly quickly. She hadn't put her bra on again and he liked the way her nipples poked against her T-shirt and her large breasts bounced as she tossed the washers.

She did a pretty good job of getting her washers close to the pipe and even got one inside it a few times. The games were close with Megan winning one game and Ryan winning two.

"You let me win that second game, didn't you," she said when he won the last game.

"It was all you, honey." He leaned over and kissed her soft lips. He pushed damp hair from her face with his thumb. "What do you say to some steaks for dinner with potatoes, corn on the cob, and a little salad?"

Something about her smile warmed him as she said, "Oh, gourmet. I say that sounds great."

He picked up the washers game and put it away while she got out the potatoes, corn on the cob, and an onion.

"Maybe we can have more s'mores later," he said with a wink.

A sexy little blush stole across her face. "S'mores sound really good…especially if it leads to another wild night of unbelievable sex."

He grinned, took her in his arms, and gave her a kiss to tell her how much he agreed.

The afternoon was cooling off as it turned to dusk and then darkness descended on them. They each grabbed a light sweat jacket from the camper and slipped them on.

Ryan took a couple of steaks out of the cooler to cook over the fire. Megan sliced the potatoes and wrapped them in foil with butter and seasonings and put them in the coals first. Ryan buttered, salted, and peppered the corn on the cob and wrapped them in foil, too. When it was time, they placed the corn along the edge of the fire. Ryan had cored out the onion and put butter in the center and wrapped it in foil and put it in the coals, as well. The steaks went on last, when everything else was just about finished cooking.

When it was ready, they sat on the camping chairs in front of the fire and ate dinner.

"This is unbelievable," Megan said with a smile.

Firelight flickered on her pretty features, casting shadows in the darkness as they ate. He thought about what he'd said to her earlier.

"I might be falling for you, Meg."

He didn't regret his words. He'd dated a lot of women in the past but there'd just been something missing. Something intangible that he hadn't been able to name.

He'd never been a love 'em and leave 'em kind of guy, but some thought so. He just wasn't going to hang in there with someone if he knew she wasn't the right one.

He'd never felt the same way with anyone that he did with Megan.

Last night he'd taken her hard and rough, and the memory caused his groin to ache. Damn she'd been amazing. But she needed to know that he wanted more from her than a night of good, hard sex.

When they finished dinner and had cleaned up, he brought a blanket from the camper and handed it to her before he put out the fire. After he extinguished the fire, he lit a candle within a glass and metal hurricane lantern.

He took her by the hand. "I've got something I want to show you." Her hand was warm in his.

She smiled up at him, her smile causing something deep inside him to stir. He led her into the forest, candlelight from the hurricane lantern lighting the way. The candlelight was much gentler than a regular camping lantern and the shadows from it bounced from tree to tree.

"I saw a place somewhere over here," he murmured as they walked through the forest then came to a stop. "Here we go."

A small clearing lay on the other side of a fallen tree, a bed of leaves at the center of the clearing. They stepped over the tree and then he found a sturdy place to set the hurricane before taking the blanket from Megan and spreading it out on the leaves.

He slipped out of his jacket and set it on the fallen tree. "I'll keep you warm," he said as he held out his hand.

She looked up at him, slid off her sweat jacket, handed it to him and he set it on top of his own.

He sat on the blanket and beckoned to her. She eased onto her knees beside him and he cupped her face in his hands and lowered his head and kissed her.

Her kiss was sweet and his desire for her kicked into full gear. He wanted to take her hard again, right now. But more importantly, he wanted to show her that it wasn't only about rough sex with him. It was all about her.

When he drew away from the kiss, her lips were parted, hunger in her pretty green eyes.

"You're an incredible woman." He brushed his thumb over her lips, which trembled beneath his touch. "I've loved every minute of this weekend."

"So have I," she said, her voice just above a whisper. "I wish it didn't have to end."

"It doesn't." He nuzzled her hair that was silky now that it had dried. "When we return, we just pick right back up where we left off."

She smiled and he kissed her again. She felt so soft and warm in his arms. He slid his hand under her T-shirt, pleased she didn't have her bra on as he cupped her bare breast and rubbed his thumb over her nipple. He watched her expression as her lips parted and her eyes grew dark with need.

He drew the T-shirt over her head and set it on the fallen tree. Candlelight flickered, gently touching her bare shoulders and chest.

"You know how much I love your body and how beautiful I think you are," he murmured before stroking her nipples with the back of his hand.

He cupped her breasts, feeling their weight in his hands before he lowered his head and sucked a nipple.

She gasped and leaned back so that her hands were braced behind her on the blanket, her back arched so that he had better access to her breasts. He pressed them together and moved his mouth from one to the other, sucking one nipple before moving his mouth to the other one. Her nipples were large and hard and he loved sucking on them.

"I want you on your back, looking at me." He adjusted her so that she was lying on the blanket. Her eyes glittered in the light, desire on her features.

He was surprised at how she made him want to go slow with her, to be gentle and show her how much he cared. She stirred things inside him he'd never felt with another woman.

Watching her features, he grasped the zipper on her jeans. He looked down as he unzipped them and revealed her sexy red lacy panties. He liked that she hadn't worn something that might be considered practical on a camping trip. He grasped one of her legs and bent it and removed her shoe and sock, then repeated with the other leg and foot.

"Raise your hips," he said when he finished and she was lying flat on her back again. She obeyed and he grasped the waistband

and pulled off her jeans.

"It's cold." She shivered as he set her jeans aside and goose bumps broke out on her skin.

"Don't worry," he murmured. "I'll warm you up."

He trailed his finger along the waistband of her lacy red panties. "You wore these for me, didn't you?"

She nodded, her silky hair sliding on the blanket.

"It's a shame to take them off," he said. "But I like the way you look completely naked." She raised her hips again as he slid her panties over her hips and down, then slipped them off. "Beautiful," he said as he lightly stroked the curls at the apex of her thighs.

"You mentioned something about warming me up," she said and held her arms out to him.

He adjusted his position and covered her body with his, careful to not put his whole weight on her. He braced his hands to either side of her head and looked down at her. "How's that?" he asked.

"It would be better if you were naked," she said with a sexy little smile.

A rumble rose up in his chest. He felt a primal rush of desire that burned beneath his skin. He could just push down his jeans and slide into her right now, the way she was. But he wanted to give her more.

He pressed her legs apart with his palms and knelt between her thighs as he pulled his T-shirt over his head. "How's that?" he said as he ran his finger down her curls toward her folds. "Better?"

"Yes." Her voice trembled. "But I want you naked."

He smiled and moved so that he could take off his athletic shoes and socks, then unzipped his jeans and slid them and his boxer briefs off. He dug into his pocket for the condom packet before tossing the jeans onto her clothing.

Despite the chill in the air, his cock was hard, primed and ready.

He went to her and knelt between her thighs. She was biting her lower lip as she looked up at him.

"Are you ready for me?" He rubbed his erection along her folds, the ache in his cock and balls so great he almost couldn't hold himself back. He just might explode if she didn't say yes. "I'm ready to be inside you."

"Yes." She nodded. "Please."

He sheathed his cock then pressed it against the entrance to her core. He watched her face as he slid deep inside her.

"You're so tight," he said as her lips parted and she gasped.

"And you're so big," she said as he started sliding in and out.

She wrapped her thighs around his hips as he took her. He liked the feel of her holding him tight as he moved at a slow, even pace. He grasped her hands in his and held them to either side of her.

So much desire was wrapped up inside him that he could barely control himself. Despite the cool air he felt sweat bead on his forehead and he clenched his jaw.

"Take me harder," she said as she squeezed his hands. "I know you want to."

He just about lost it and almost started pounding into her. He managed to control himself but increased his pace.

Her chest rose and fell as her breathing escalated.

His strokes increased as he took her a little faster, then a little faster yet. An orgasm built inside him until he was almost ready to explode.

The candlelight played over her features as her eyes grew wider and her breaths came in short bursts.

"Come, baby," he murmured. "Come with me."

She cried out a moment later, her body bowing, and her cry sent him over the edge. His orgasm burst through him, spreading from his groin outward, sending heat through his body and he growled out his release as he cried out her name.

Her core clamped down on him as he throbbed inside her. He managed a few more strokes and then he pressed himself tight against her.

He brought her into his arms and rolled them both to the side where he kept her in his embrace.

"You were right," she said.

He brushed damp strands from her forehead. "About what?"

"You warmed me right up."

He smiled and kissed her, and held her tightly.

CHAPTER 16

Sunday morning, they packed up camp and headed back to civilization. As Ryan drove, Megan leaned back in the truck's passenger seat and smiled at him.

"Thank you again for taking me." She reached for his hand on the console and he laced his fingers with hers. "That was one of the best times I can remember having. Ever."

"I'm right there with you." He smiled and glanced at her as he steered. "That was the best camping trip I've been on, and I've been on a lot of camping trips."

The words he'd spoken to her yesterday at the lake slipped in to her consciousness.

I might be falling for you, Meg.

The memory sent a delighted shiver through her body. She

was falling for him, and fast, but she wasn't ready to tell him that. She was too afraid of getting hurt once again.

When they got within cell phone range, Megan grabbed her small purse from beneath the passenger seat and pulled out her phone. She pressed the power button but the phone wouldn't turn on.

"I must have forgotten to charge my phone before I left," she said. "The battery is dead."

"Just as well," he said. "There's something about camping and getting away from all of the electronic stuff anyway."

She smiled at him. "It's going to be hard going back to the real world."

"Who says we have to get back to the real world?" He gave her a quick grin. "How about dinner tonight?"

She laughed. "I have a date with a nice long hot bath tonight where there are no bears."

With a teasing look he said, "I have a tub."

"And if we end up in it I'll never get any rest and I have to get back to work in the morning." She tilted her head to the side and smiled at him. "Although it would be worth it."

She felt a little sleepy as he drove, exhausted from the long weekend. Yet part of her felt exhilarated too from having an fantastic time with Ryan.

When they reached his ranch, she helped him unload the camper and clean it up. She took out the bedding and carried it to his laundry room and started the wash as he put away the fishing rods and tackle.

They made a good team as they went to work and it didn't take them long at all before the camper was clean and everything was put away. When they were finished, he parked the camper inside a big shop at the back of the house then returned to her car.

She tossed her duffel in the passenger seat when they were finished and he walked with her to the driver's side of the car. He opened the door for her then put his hands on her waist and lowered his head to kiss her.

His kisses never failed to stir flames inside her. He slowly moved his mouth over hers and she sighed with a kind of happiness she'd never remembered experiencing before.

As he drew away she smiled. "Wow. I might never go home if you keep that up."

"Good." He brought his lips close to hers. "If you need any more convincing I'm up for it."

She gave him a solid kiss and drew away. "Okay, mister. I'd better get on home."

He grinned and stepped back. "I'll give you a call and we can figure out dinner this week."

"Sounds like a good plan to me." She eased into the driver's seat and buzzed down the window as he closed the Camry's door. "Thank you," she said as she looked up at him. "Thank you for the most incredible weekend ever."

"It took the two of us together." He smiled. "Be careful driving home and get some rest. You're going to need it."

"Oh, yeah?" She raised a brow.

He nodded. "I'll see to it."

With a grin she started the car and backed up. She blew him a kiss before buzzing the window up, turning the car around, and heading down the road.

As she drove she hummed and pulled her cell phone out of

her purse. She managed to connect it to the charger and let the phone rest in a cup holder as she drove toward town.

The happiness bubbling up inside her made her feel as if she should be dancing. She turned on the radio and one of her favorite old songs, *I'm So Excited* by the Pointer Sisters, was playing. It fit her mood perfectly. She might be tone deaf, but she sang her heart out at the top of her lungs.

About ten minutes after leaving Ryan's house, her phone beeped, telling her she had a message. The phone was apparently charged enough now to use. While keeping one hand on the wheel, she glanced at the LCD display.

"Twelve new voice mail messages?" She said to herself. Was everything okay at home?

She raised the phone to her ear and listened to the first message from last night, Saturday.

"Megan." It was her mother's distraught voice. "We think your father had a heart attack. The paramedics had to revive him and rush him to the hospital."

A wash of cold went through Megan. Heart pounding, she listened to the next message. "Dad's had a heart attack," Tess said and Megan's skin grew colder. "He's in critical condition. Come as soon as you get this message."

The next ten messages were her mother's frantic calls and her sister's updates. Tess was calmer than their mother but the urgency was there. Their father was in ICU after undergoing emergency surgery, and his condition hadn't improved.

Megan hit the speed dial number for Tess.

"Megan," Tess answered on the first ring. "Thank God. You need to get to the hospital as soon as you can."

"I'm on my way." Megan glanced at the clock, her heart pounding. "Tell me what happened."

Tess's voice sounded teary. "Dad opened up the mail while Mom was making dinner last night. He said, 'The bastard has started foreclosure proceedings.' Dad read the notice to Mom. Then he clutched his chest and collapsed. He fell from the chair to the floor."

"Dear God," Megan said, her mind racing.

"The doctor said he had a heart attack," Tess said. "It could have been from the stress caused by the contents of that letter, among other things. He hasn't recovered from the surgery he went through last night."

Tears burned at the backs of Megan's eyes, but she held them back. Her father was still alive. He could still recover.

"How's Jenny doing?" Megan asked Tess.

"She's with Mrs. Webb," Tess said. "I've told her that her grandpa is sick and in the hospital. She's too young to tell her more. She wants to see him but they won't let children into the ICU."

"From the sound of her messages, Mom doesn't sound like she's holding up really well," Megan said.

"She's right here," Tess said. "She wants to talk to you."

"Megan?" came Margaret's voice. "Are you almost here?"

"I'm not too far now."

"They're saying he might not make it." So much fear was in Margaret's tone that Megan's stomach felt queasy. "I don't know what I'll do without him."

"He'll pull through, Mom." Megan clenched her fingers around the phone. "We have to believe that."

"I pray you're right." Margaret sounded so distressed that Megan's heart hurt.

"I'll see you soon," Megan said, praying she was right, too.

The drive to Prescott seemed to take forever. By the time Megan reached the hospital, her nerves were frayed.

She rushed into the hospital and was directed to the waiting room where her mother and Tess were.

"Mom." Megan hurried to her mother and hugged her. Margaret's eyes were red and swollen, her skin pale and features drawn. She wore a blouse and skirt as she usually did, but her normally pressed clothing was wrinkled and her makeup had been cried away.

The moment Megan brought Margaret into her arms, her mother started crying again.

Megan looked over her shoulder at Tess. "Have you heard anything new?"

"Nothing." Tess shook her head. Her eyes were red, too, and she looked exhausted. "Last we heard he's still in critical condition."

Megan rubbed her mother's back as she and Tess spoke. "Have you both been here all night?"

Tess nodded. "I tried to get Mom to sleep on the chairs but she wouldn't."

"Have you gotten any sleep?" Megan asked her sister.

Tess pushed her hand through her hair. "I guess I'm as guilty as Mom. I couldn't sleep if I tried. I'm too worried about Dad."

Megan and Tess spent the next two hours comforting Margaret. The time seemed to go by interminably slow.

The doctor finally walked in, carrying a clipboard. Margaret pulled away from Tess who'd had her arm around her. Their mother straightened and raised her chin, clearly trying to compose herself for the doctor.

"How is he, Dr. Marston?" Margaret asked, her voice hoarse from exhaustion and tears despite her attempts at composure.

"We're only twenty-six hours into it after his bypass surgery and the first forty-eight hours are the most critical." The doctor looked grim as he spoke. "He's a very sick man. His blood pressure is low and his heart is weakened but it is not damaged so much that he could not live with it. As I say though, we just don't know yet."

He continued, "We may be able to let you see him later today. The nurse will inform you if and when you can."

Margaret nodded but looked like she was going to fall apart again and grasped Megan's wrist. She pulled down on Megan's arm, as if she might collapse, and Megan adjusted herself so she could put her arm around her mother to support her.

"Thank you," Margaret said.

When the doctor left, Margaret looked from Tess to Megan. "What will I do without Paul if he—if he—if he dies?"

The words seemed to take even more out of Margaret and Megan led her back to a chair and had her sit down.

"Don't think that way, Mom." Tess sat beside Margaret. "He's going to be all right."

Margaret shook her head. "I don't know what I would do without him."

Megan had never seen her mother in such stark pain. She'd never realized just how important her parents were to each other. She knew that they loved each other, but it had never occurred to her that they would love each other so much that they couldn't exist without one another.

"Relax, Mom." Megan moved so that her mother's head was on her shoulder. "He just needs some time to heal and he'll be okay."

Margaret said, "I pray to God you're right."

CHAPTER 17

Tess sat with Margaret after Megan had held her for at least an hour. Megan got up from her seat and flexed her shoulders to get out the cramp that had developed in her arm from holding her mother for so long.

It occurred to her that she hadn't called Ryan. She needed to hear his voice.

She moved away from her mother and sister and dialed his number.

"Hi, sexy," he said as he answered

Megan hesitated as she felt tears prick at the back of her eyes. "Hi," she said.

"What's wrong?" Apparently he heard the hesitancy and concern in that one word. "Did something happen?"

"My father had a heart attack last night."

"How is he doing?" Concern was in Ryan's voice.

"The doctor isn't sure he's going to pull through." Megan held back a sob. "But there is a chance. The next forty-eight hours are critical."

"I'll be right there, Meg," he said.

Surprise made her blink. "You don't have to come."

"Yeah, I do," he said. "I care about you and I need to be there for you."

She took a deep breath. "Thank you." She told him to call her when he reached the hospital and she'd take him back to the waiting room they were in.

"I'll see you in less than an hour," he said.

She paced the room for the next hour as Tess held their mother. Megan chewed her nails as she paced, something she had started doing when Bart left her, but that she hadn't done since her divorce.

When her phone vibrated, she looked at the display and saw that it was Ryan.

"Are you here?" she answered.

"I'm at the information desk," he said.

Megan disconnected the call and looked at Tess. "I'll be right back."

Tess nodded but said nothing.

Megan headed downstairs to the information desk and saw Ryan standing there, so tall and solid. She rushed to him and he took her into his arms and held her.

"Thank you for coming," she said as she felt the heat of his body and breathed in his comforting scent.

He rocked her to him. "Are you all right?"

"As well as I can be." A tear trickled down her face as she looked up at Ryan. "He could die."

Ryan brushed the tear away with his thumb. "We'll pray for the best."

She hugged him again, burying her face against his chest as she felt his strong arms around her.

"I'd better get back to my sister and my mom," she said as she drew away.

"I'll go with you," he said. "If that's all right with you."

"It will be nice to have you here if you can stay for a little while." She wiped tears away with her fingertips. "I hope this isn't taking away time you need to spend on the ranch."

"No," he said. "You're more important."

He held her hand as they went to the elevator and rode up to the waiting room. When they entered the waiting room, Ryan put his arms around Megan's shoulders in a way that comforted her, supported her.

She started to introduce him to Tess and Margaret but Tess had a strange expression on her face.

"You'd better go," Tess said in a hard but calm tone.

"What?" Megan looked at her sister, confused, as Tess stared at Ryan.

At the same time, Margaret raised her head and followed Tess's gaze.

Margaret stiffened in Tess's arms.

"It's your fault!" Margaret screamed as she pulled away from Tess. Margaret pointed at Ryan. "Your fault he might die!"

Shock tore through Megan as she looked from her mother's

expression of hatred and turned back to Ryan. "What's going on?" Megan asked.

"Get out of here." Margaret kept shouting. "Get out of here!"

"He's the man who's foreclosing on Mom and Dad," Tess said to Megan. To Ryan she repeated, "You'd better go."

"Paul is your father? I had no idea. I'm so sorry." Ryan met Megan's gaze.

She just stared at him, unable to say anything. Paul? He knew her father?

A nurse rushed in as Margaret kept screaming.

"We'd better talk about this," Ryan said to Megan. He backed up then turned away and went out the waiting room doors.

Stunned, Megan stared at the doors as Margaret sobbed and the nurse tried to calm her.

Megan looked at Tess. "Ryan is foreclosing on them?" She was still having a hard time connecting the fact that the man she had just spent the weekend with was the same man who was causing her family so much distress.

"He came to their restaurant a week ago Thursday and told them they had to make the balloon payment because he was going to file." Tess held their mom and rubbed her back. "Mom, it's okay."

Thursday. Ryan had the talk with her parents the same day she'd met him.

"It's not okay." Margaret raised her head, her face tear-stained. She narrowed her gaze at Megan. "What was Ryan McBride doing here?"

"He's the man I went camping with," Megan said slowly.

Both Margaret's and Tess's eyes widened. "You went camping with *him*?"

"I didn't know he was the one foreclosing on you." Megan shook her head. "If I'd known, I would never have dated him."

"You've been dating him?" Tess asked. "He would have known our parents' names."

"He was using you to get to us," Margaret said with a fierce expression.

"He didn't know anything about you." Megan rubbed her palms on her jeans, her mind still whirling with confusion. "I didn't tell him who my family was."

"Oh, he knew," Margaret said in a biting tone. "Why else would he have been going out with you?"

Megan felt like she'd been slapped. Her mother's words cut deeply, as if Megan couldn't attract a man like Ryan.

But had he known? Was that why he'd approached her?

"She didn't mean it that way," Tess said as their mother walked away from the nurse and started moving around the room as if lost.

"Yes, she did." Megan looked from Tess to watch their mother. "You know she did."

Tess didn't say anything. What could she say?

As for Ryan, Megan didn't know what to think or how to handle it. It didn't seem real that he was the reason her father was in the hospital, the reason he'd had a heart attack. And that Ryan was the man trying to take their home away.

Tears backed up behind her eyes. She'd just had the most amazing weekend of her life. Had it all been a lie?

How could she see him anymore? She wouldn't see him. Look what he'd done to her family.

She wanted to sit down, bury her face in her hands, and cry.

The pain she felt in her heart was like she'd been stabbed with a knife and her mother had twisted the blade.

Another nurse walked into the room as she looked at Margaret. "Mr. Dyson is awake and wants to see you."

Margaret headed for the door, her steps quick and rushed.

The nurse looked at Megan and Tess. "Are you both his daughters?"

"Yes," Tess said and Megan nodded.

"He wants to see you, too." The nurse opened the door for Margaret to walk through. "You can go in one at a time. You each can have five minutes, no more than that. He's weak and we can't risk exhausting him." When Margaret was through the door, the nurse said, "I'll be back for you when it's your turn."

The nurse who had been consoling their mother left, too. Megan rubbed her arms with both of her hands, trying to chase away a chill that wouldn't leave her body.

Her mind bounced back and forth between the revelation that Ryan had been the one to cause her family distress, and the fact that her father could die.

Anger made her throb so hard it ached. How could he have been so horrible?

It didn't jive with the man she'd gotten to know who had been so popular with almost everyone they'd come into contact with who knew him. The only one who hadn't been cordial was the drunk who had been trying to start a fight with another man the night she and Ryan had gone out to dinner.

Could Ryan have approached her because he knew who she was? It didn't make sense. What purpose would that have served?

And this weekend… Everything had been so real, so wonderful. She didn't think Ryan had been faking any of it.

Yet a niggling of doubt kept knocking at her brain.

Doubt followed by anger over what he'd done to their family.

Even though it hadn't been more than six or seven minutes since Margaret had walked out of the room, it seemed to take forever for her mother to return.

"He doesn't look good." Margaret's eyes were glossy with tears. "Don't mention that bastard being here, either one of you. And don't tell him that you've been seeing him, Megan," Margaret said as she looked accusingly at Megan. "He's weak and that might kill him."

"Of course not, Mom." Tess spoke gently. "I'll go next," she said to Megan, then left with the nurse.

While Tess was in with their father, Megan paced the floor as her mother sat in a chair and sobbed. Every now and then Margaret would say words like, "It's all that bastard's fault," and to Megan, "How could you have been seeing him? How could you do that to this family?"

Once again, Megan didn't try to defend herself, she just took what was thrown at her. She did her best not to let her mother slice through her with words. She'd grown up with the verbal abuse and had married someone who had done the same thing.

She'd thought Ryan was different, that he would never hurt her. But he couldn't be the man she'd thought he was if he could do something like this to her family when they were hurting so badly for money. He could have worked something out with them, but instead he was foreclosing on their home.

Tess returned and walked into the room. Her eyes were red but dry, as if she was forcing back tears. She didn't say anything, just went to their mother and brought her into her arms.

The nurse held the door open for Megan. She looked back at her mother and sister, then followed the nurse out the door.

Her stomach twisted as they walked from the waiting room, down a hall, and through a pair of doors that led to the ICU. The journey seemed so long even though it wasn't that far.

The antiseptic smell of the hospital and the sounds of beeps on monitors surrounded her. The nurse led her past a nurse's station to a room with windows, but the curtains were drawn.

"No more than five minutes," the nurse reminded her. "I'll come and get you when your time is up. But if he seems to get worse, I'll be waiting outside."

Megan nodded and walked into the room. She fought back tears the moment she saw her father. She didn't want him to see her crying—she needed to be strong for him.

The man who'd always seemed so big to her now looked shrunken and pale against a backdrop of monitors and machines. One of them showed his heartbeat. She didn't know anything about heart monitors beyond what she'd seen on TV, but to her his heartbeat seemed weak.

She walked toward him, noticing that his breathing seemed shallow and he made a wheezing sound.

"Megan." He held up the hand with the IV in it and gestured to her to come closer. Her feet felt so heavy, her body stiff as she went to him.

When she reached his side, she slipped her hand into his. "Hi, Dad," she said, barely able to get the words out. "How are you doing?" she said, then added, "Other than the fact that you had a heart attack and you're in the hospital."

He gave an attempt at a smile. "I'm not going to last much longer."

"Don't say that." It was harder to fight back tears now and she had to bite the inside of her lip. When she could talk without her voice wavering, she said, "You're going to be okay, Dad."

His throat worked as he swallowed. "I want to say a few things to you."

She held his hand in both of hers. "I can tell that you need to rest. Then we can talk."

"I haven't been the best father to you, Megan." He winced as he spoke, as if he'd felt a stab of pain. He focused on her again. "I want you to know how proud of you I am. You're a beautiful woman and I should never have been so hard on you."

Prickles covered Megan from head to toe. Her father had never told her he was proud of her. Ever.

"Trust your judgment," her father said. "I've always second guessed you and I shouldn't have. You have had good judgment throughout your life. I just needed to let go sooner but I guess I was always afraid to."

He continued, "Throughout your life I've been hard on you," he said, his voice weak. "But I've wanted the best for you."

A tear leaked down her cheek. She didn't know what to say.

"I shouldn't have let your mother be so hard on you." He looked sad. "Between the two of us, things probably weren't easy for you in our household."

"Don't worry about anything right now." She gripped his hand. "You need to get better."

He wheezed before he said, "I want you to know that I love you, Megan."

Another tear rolled down her face. "I love you, Dad."

He closed his eyes like it was too difficult for him to continue talking.

She squeezed his hand. "Get some rest."

Just as she started to walk away, something started blaring. Her heart jerked. She looked at the monitor and saw that he had flatlined. She sucked in her breath, feeling like her own heart stopped at the same moment.

The nurse rushed in and checked the monitor then called for assistance. Megan felt like cotton was in her ears and she couldn't hear as fear went through her.

Someone took hold of her arm and spoke, a nurse, but Megan couldn't grasp what she was saying. The nurse spoke louder and Megan barely heard, "We need you out."

She was escorted out of her father's room while nurses and a doctor rushed in.

Megan was taken back to the waiting area. As soon as she walked through the door, Margaret and Tess looked at her with fear in their expressions.

It must have been on her face because Tess rushed to her. "Dad? Is he okay?"

"He flatlined." Megan's words stuck in her throat. "They're working on him now."

"No." The word came out of Margaret on a sob as she sank into a chair. "Nooo."

Megan and Tess waited on either side of their mother. Tess had her arm around Margaret and Megan held one of her hands.

It wasn't much longer before a doctor came through the door, a grim look on his face.

Margaret got to her feet and Tess and Megan stood as well. "Tell me Paul is all right," Margaret said as if demanding that the doctor give her good news.

"I'm sorry, Mrs. Dyson," the doctor said. "His heart gave out. I'm afraid he's gone."

Margaret's knees buckled but Tess and Megan caught her before she fell. Megan looked at her face and saw that her mother had fainted.

Megan felt numb as the doctor rushed to Margaret's side. A nurse handed the doctor something that he put under Margaret's nose, causing her to suck in her breath and open her eyes. She was helped into a chair and checked over as Tess and Megan watched.

Tess gripped Megan's arm. "He's really dead?"

Megan felt tears roll down her cheeks as she looked at her sister. "Yes. He's gone."

Tess broke down, crying in Megan's arms. Megan closed her eyes, unable to believe her father was no longer with them.

CHAPTER 18

The night of their father's death, Margaret checked out mentally. Five days later, she didn't seem to be any better.

Megan had always thought of her mother as a strong person both emotionally and physically. She never expected Margaret to seem to vanish. She was there, but she wasn't.

At the hospital, after their father had passed on, out of the three of them, Megan had been the most capable at that moment of dealing with the hospital and the paperwork. Tess tried to console their mother while they both cried. Margaret signed the papers wherever Megan told her to.

When they'd reached their parents' house, Tess and Megan made their mother lie down in her bed. Margaret simply stared at the ceiling. She wouldn't respond to anything they said.

After they'd put a blanket on Margaret and tucked it around her, Tess and Megan had done their best to console each other and check in on their mother from time to time.

Over the past few days, Megan had taken care funeral arrangements and Tess had handled the restaurant, closing it temporarily until their mother checked back into reality. If Margaret didn't recover soon, Megan and Tess would have to decide what to do with the restaurant.

After working with her parents for years, Tess had experience running a restaurant, so she could take her mother's place, but she would need a good cook and a waitress and would need to be able to pay them competitive wages. Tess and Megan needed to dig into the restaurant's finances and get things straight before they opened the restaurant again.

Then there was the foreclosure looming over them. But they would have to wait to deal with that.

Megan's heart squeezed and her belly cramped as she thought about Ryan. The pain she'd felt over losing him had been almost more than she could bear. It was like something was tearing her apart inside, ripping her to shreds. She'd never thought it could hurt so much to love someone and lose him.

Love. *No.* It couldn't be love.

But what else could be so powerful it nearly drove her to her knees?

He had called at least once a day, but she had ignored his calls and deleted his voice messages before listening to them. She deleted his text messages, too, but couldn't avoid seeing parts of them, like "please let me explain," and "I'm not letting you go that easily."

Every time she saw a message from him the tears would start

again. She had to struggle to keep it together.

A part of her wanted to text back or take the calls, but how could she? Not after all that he'd done. She just couldn't.

The morning of the funeral, Jenny was again with Mrs. Webb while Tess and Megan tried to get prepared.

When they needed a moment to talk, Megan and Tess went into the kitchen to make some hot blackberry tea, something that had always soothed them in the past. Not that it would be able to make them feel better now, but it was a ritual that helped to calm them. They sat at the table drinking tea after offering Margaret some, but their mother was as unresponsive as she had been the day their father had died.

"How did you meet Ryan McBride?" Tess asked quietly as they sat at the table, catching Megan off guard.

She felt a twist in her belly at the mention of Ryan's name. They hadn't talked about him since everything else had happened. She remained quiet for a moment. She didn't want to revisit anything but at the same time she wanted to talk about him.

The pain of her father's loss, and of learning about Ryan's actions contributing to the heart attack, made her chest hurt as if she was having a heart attack herself.

"We met at the county fair." Megan ran her finger along the rim of the hot porcelain teacup. "You hadn't shown up and he introduced himself to me. When I got the message that you and Jenny couldn't make it, I agreed to spend the day with him." Megan squeezed her eyes shut for a moment. "I don't want to believe he knew who I am."

Tess sighed. "Don't listen to Mom. She's always been too hard on you. Sunday was worse because of what happened to Dad and she said some things she shouldn't have."

"What if she's right?" Megan clenched her hand on the table-top. "What if Ryan was trying to use me in some way?"

Tess shook her head. "It makes no sense. How could he use you to get to Mom and Dad? Mom was just freaking out."

"Of course you're right." Megan slid her finger into the teacup handle. "But why me? Why did he pick me at the fair?"

"You're a beautiful woman inside and out." Tess wrapped her hands around her teacup as if warming them. "I'm sure he was attracted to what he saw."

"I have such a hard time reconciling the Ryan I'd gotten to know with the one who's taking away my family's home." Megan met her sister's gaze. "He was fun and kind, and seemed popular with kids and adults wherever we went."

"How well did you get to know him?" Tess asked.

Megan looked down at her hot tea. "As well as any couple could."

"I'm sorry." Tess reached out and covered Megan's hand with her own. "What are you going to do now?"

Megan sipped her tea and set the cup down. "It's over, of course."

"You really care for him," Tess said.

"Too much." Megan rubbed her eyes with her thumb and forefinger. "I was falling for him so hard... I think I did fall for him." She looked at Tess and held her hand to her chest. "It hurts. It's like I lost not only my father, but someone else I cared for." She had cried countless tears, not only for the loss of her father, but for Ryan, too.

"Aw, honey." Tess rubbed her hand along Megan's arm. "I

didn't realize it was that serious."

"It wasn't—it's not—it's—" Megan bit her lower lip. "I don't know what it is."

"You're in love with him," Tess said quietly.

"I can't be in love with him." Megan shook her head. "Look what he's done."

"Dad would have had the heart attack eventually, you know that." Tess took a deep breath. "The doctor said it was just waiting to happen and that it was probably a coincidence."

Megan frowned at her sister. "Why are you defending Ryan now? You were just as angry with him as Mom and Dad have been."

Tess paused as if thinking over her words. "Because if you care for him then there's something there that's good."

"Yeah, I've got a great track record." Megan gave an unlady-like snort. "Just look at Bart."

"There's good in Bart," Tess said and Megan looked at her with surprise. "At least there was. Unfortunately, he was eventually won over by the Dark Side."

Megan frowned. "I'm not so sure I'm keeping up with your logic."

"What's he like?" Tess asked.

Megan thought about Ryan and the wonderful times they'd had. "He's well-liked, friendly, fun, caring."

Tess rested her elbow on the table and put her chin in her hand. "Did he treat you well?"

Megan couldn't help a smile. "No one has ever treated me better. He was sweet and attentive, yet he's a real man's man."

"Mom and Dad have a different way of looking at things," Tess said. "Just maybe they were all wrong about Ryan." Tess folded her hands on the table. "If he's as good of a guy as he sounds, you need to give him another chance."

With a sigh, Megan said, "I don't know."

"Older sisters know best," Tess said. "And I say you should talk to him."

"No fair pulling out the Older Sister card." Megan looked up at the clock. "It's time to get ready for the funeral."

"Hopefully we can get Mom to pull herself together for it," Tess said with a sigh.

Between the two of them, they were able to get Margaret dressed in a simple black sheath dress and black heels. Tess had bought a stylish hat for their mother with a veil that came down just below the eyes so that no one could easily see her vacant stare.

"I'm still having a hard time with Jenny going to her grandfather's funeral," Tess said to Megan before Mrs. Webb arrived with her daughter. "It's hard enough letting it sink in myself."

"I understand." Megan nodded. Even five days later she was still having a difficult time coming to terms with the fact that her father was dead, much less having had to sit down with a five-year-old and explain that someone she loved had died.

When Mrs. Webb arrived, Jenny came rushing in, carrying her doll with the frizzy blonde ponytail and one eye glued shut. Instead of the doll being naked as usual, she was wearing a little white dress with black polka dots, and the doll had a black ribbon around her ponytail.

Jenny threw herself into her mother's arms. Tess picked up her daughter and hugged her tightly.

As Tess set her down on the floor, Jenny held her doll tightly in one arm. "Mrs. Webb made Bette a new dress." She held her doll up with both hands, presenting Bette to her mother. "Isn't she pretty?"

"I see that." Tess looked like she was holding back tears. "She's very pretty. How about we get you dressed, too?"

Jenny pointed to Mrs. Webb who was holding a plastic bag over a hanger. "Mrs. Webb made me a dress that matches Bette's."

"Thank you, Mrs. Webb." Tess gave the older lady a kiss on the cheek. "You're wonderful."

"Are you going to be all right, Miss Tess?" She enveloped Tess in a big hug.

When they parted, Tess sniffled and wiped a tear from here eye. "Eventually," she said. Mrs. Webb had become like family to Tess and Jenny.

Mrs. Webb turned to Megan. "What about you, Miss Megan?"

"It's hard," Megan replied. "It will take a while."

"Of course it will." Mrs. Webb patted her shoulder. "Is there anything I can do for you girls?"

Tess and Megan both shook their heads. "Thank you," Megan said and Tess spoke in kind.

"Where are we going, Mommy?" Jenny asked.

"I'll explain as we get you dressed," Tess said.

When Jenny was finished dressing, she indeed matched Bette and wore a white dress with black polka dots and black bows in her hair. She wore shiny black Mary Jane's and white socks.

Every pew in the small church filled after Megan, Margaret, Tess, Mrs. Webb, and Jenny, carrying Bette, had arrived. It was a church her father and mother had belonged to over the past year since arriving in Prescott.

Megan hadn't realized how many people her parents had

come to know since moving to this town. Fellow churchgoers, business owners they had worked with, loyal patrons, and neighbors came to pay their respects.

When the casket was carried into the church, Megan turned to watch the procession.

A jolt went through her when she saw Ryan standing in the very back, against the wall. He wore a cream-colored dress shirt; black western dress pants; polished black boots; and was holding a black western hat. He watched the pallbearers and didn't meet her gaze. She wasn't sure if he realized she'd seen him. He'd come to pay his respects to her father.

She turned away and faced the pastor at the front of the church. Tears rolled down her cheeks as she listened to him give the eulogy. A ringing in her ears made it hard to hear as she felt the gut-wrenching emptiness that was left in place of the man who had been her father. Two men whom Megan had never met stood and spoke, each saying in their own way that her father was a good man and that they had been fortunate to know him.

She turned once during the service and saw that Ryan had sat down in the last row, but as the service ended and the exit procession started, he left.

When it was time to go to the cemetery, the pallbearers carried the casket to the hearse parked outside. Megan and her family followed down the aisle, a part of the procession as they headed to the waiting limo.

As they proceeded, Megan thought about her father's last words and the gift he'd given to her. She had been able to forgive him and not hold on to the resentment that had been in her heart.

CHAPTER 19

Two days after the funeral, Tess told Megan she wanted to go for a drive in the afternoon, that there were things she wanted to talk about. They'd left Jenny with Mrs. Webb, who was also taking care of Margaret.

Their mother had started a slow journey back to reality and Megan was relieved that she was coming back to them.

The day was sunny, the rainy weather having passed on.

"Have you called him yet?" Tess asked as she drove through town.

"Ryan?" Megan asked.

Tess rolled her eyes at Megan. "No. Santa Claus. Who else?"

"No, I haven't talked with St. Nick or Ryan either, for that matter." Megan shook her head. "But he has tried to call and text."

"Then we're going." Tess turned onto the highway leading out of town.

"What?" Megan looked at her sister. "Where are we going?"

"I think you should give Ryan a chance to say whatever it is he has to say." Tess looked straight ahead at the highway.

Megan narrowed her gaze. "Tess..."

"I pulled the Older Sister card, remember?" Tess kept her eyes on the highway.

"So what are you saying?" Megan said slowly.

"I think in your heart you want to talk to Ryan." Tess finally looked at Megan. "You need to talk to him."

Megan looked out the window. "Where are we going?" she asked again.

Tess bit her lower lip. "Don't be mad at me."

Megan's heart started pounding. "Tess..."

Tess looked apologetic as she pulled the car off the highway and onto a dirt road.

The road that led to Ryan's ranch.

Megan widened her eyes. "You turn this car right around."

Tess had both hands on the wheel as her car shimmied down the dirt road toward Ryan's place. "I've always been protective of you, Megan. But I want you to be happy too. I guess what I'm hoping is that maybe there is a valid explanation and you can have a happy ever after."

Megan stared out the window at the passing scenery, nerves suddenly twisting her belly. "As if there is such a thing."

"Before Steve died, I believed in it." Tess's voice was quiet. "I don't know if I'll ever find a man I could love as much as I loved Steve. I'm not sure I want to."

"Steve was a great guy." Megan felt a wave of sadness for her sister. "You have Jenny and that has to help."

Tess smiled. "Jenny is our blessing. She reminds me so much of her father. He was a good man."

"Yes, he was," Megan said. "I would love to find someone as special as Steve."

Tess met Megan's gaze. "Ryan might be that man."

"I don't know." Megan pushed hair from her eyes. "I just don't know what to think anymore." She clenched her fists on her lap. "I don't know if this is a good idea. I've ignored his calls and messages."

"Stop second guessing yourself. He'll want to talk to you," Tess said. "I saw him at the funeral and he sent flowers, too."

Megan's stomach jolted as they crossed the cattle guard and she saw Ryan's truck. Tess drove up the driveway and pulled her Honda Accord next to Ryan's vehicle and parked.

Tess looked at Megan. "You're not mad at me, are you?"

Megan tried to be mad at her sister but couldn't be. Still she said, "I'm still thinking about whether or not I want to strangle you right now."

The corners of Tess's lips tipped up in a smile. "I knew you wanted to talk with him. You just needed a little push."

"You're coming with me, right?" Megan looked at Tess. "After all, this was your idea."

"I'd like the opportunity to meet him." Tess stared at the house. "Size him up."

"Haven't you met him at the restaurant when he's stopped by?" Megan asked.

"Not really." Tess unfastened her seat belt. "I've seen him go into the kitchen to talk with Dad, but I never had the chance to meet him. Dad always came out raving mad after Ryan left, so all I have are negative images of him."

"So, what makes you think he's okay now?" Megan asked.

"You know how negative our parents are and how worked up Dad would get over things." Tess looked thoughtful. "Maybe there was more to it than what we saw."

Megan thought about the man she'd gotten to know. Was she being too hard on him? Maybe she needed to trust her own judgment like her father had said.

Out loud she said, "But he was foreclosing on our parents and not trying to work anything out with them. Something just isn't right about that."

"Well, you'll get your chance to talk to him." Tess nodded in the direction of the corrals.

Megan followed her gaze and her heart jerked in her chest as Ryan reached them, pulling his horse to a stop. The horse had a red coat with a black mane, tail, and socks.

But the horse wasn't really what she was looking at. Ryan had her attention.

He didn't have a shirt on, just jeans low-slung at his hips, worn boots, and a white straw western hat. In that one moment she remembered him taking her rough and hard the first night and how much that had excited her. In the next moment she thought about his gentleness on the blanket in the forest beneath candlelight.

She shook her head, rattling the thoughts around in her brain.

"Go on," Tess said quietly.

Megan unfastened her seatbelt and started to open the car door. Ryan had already dismounted and was there, opening it for her.

He took her hand and she felt the familiar connection between them as he helped her out of the car. And then they were face to face, their eyes locked, neither of them saying a word.

The incredible weekend they'd had together came rushing through her mind. Not just the sex, but fishing, hiking, skinny-dipping, and so much more.

And then he brought her into his arms and hugged her tight. She felt the tension and emotion rushing from her body.

"Hi." Tess's voice jerked Megan out of her trance and she stepped out of his embrace. "I'm Tess." She held her hand out and Ryan turned to her and took it.

"Ryan McBride." He released her hand and touched the brim of his hat. "A pleasure to meet you, Tess."

She studied him. "Don't hurt Megan or you'll have me to answer to."

Megan's jaw dropped.

The five-foot-three woman staring up at the six-foot-one muscular man and warning him off would have been amusing if it wasn't for the dead serious look in her eyes.

"You have nothing to worry about, Tess." Ryan spoke with a seriousness in his voice that surprised Megan. "I would never hurt her."

Tess gave him one last look then turned her gaze on Megan. "I'm going to get back to town to check on Mom. Are you okay with me leaving you? Something tells me you won't have a problem getting a ride home."

Megan's jaw dropped. "You can't leave me here."

"I'll get you home safely," Ryan said.

Megan felt trapped. Tess had brought her out to talk to Ryan and was now leaving her alone with the man. She'd feel like a total idiot if she insisted on leaving now with Tess. It would be completely immature. It wasn't the same as ignoring his calls.

Was it?

Neither Ryan nor Megan said anything as Tess got into her car. She waved as she backed up, then turned the car around and drove away from the ranch house.

Megan was almost afraid to look at Ryan. She closed her eyes then opened them again.

"Meg?" He rested his hand on her upper arm. "Talk to me."

"I don't know why Tess brought me here." She turned to face him. "My Dad had a heart attack while reading the letter that you were foreclosing on him. I'm not sure there's anything to talk about."

"I'm sorry about your dad." Ryan's eyes were shadowed by the brim of his hat.

"So am I." Her father's last words went through her mind.

I want you to know how proud of you I am.

Why had he waited to say those words until just moments before he'd died?

"I know you're hurting," Ryan said. "But will you let me explain?"

He held her gaze a long moment and then she nodded. "I don't see how that will help, but go ahead."

"The house your parents bought isn't mine so I'm not the one foreclosing on them," Ryan said.

Megan frowned. "What do you mean?"

Ryan pushed up the brim of his hat and she could see the blue of his eyes. "It belongs to my uncle and aunt."

"Your uncle and aunt?" she said slowly.

"I owe my uncle a favor and I've been trying to work everything out to help them." Ryan took off his hat and pushed his hand through his hair before setting his hat back on his head.

"Your parents bought the house," Ryan continued, "and my uncle financed it because it wasn't the right time for a loan for your parents for some reason. They were to either refinance the house by now or make a large balloon payment. They have done neither. My uncle is counting on that balloon payment to make his finances work or he might lose his ranch."

Megan's skin prickled. "Is that why you won't try to work something out with my parents?"

"I talked with my uncle and tried to get him to break it down into smaller payments, but he refused." Ryan looked frustrated. "He's a stubborn man. But at the same time, I understand because they do need the money."

"My parents said you were harsh and they made it sound like you were a real jerk," she said.

"I hope you know me better than to believe I would treat your parents in any way but respectful." Ryan studied Megan. "They were angry with me, the messenger. I tried to discuss it with them and they wouldn't hear of it. Your father said flatly that they couldn't make the balloon payment. He said they'd continue making payments on the house, but my uncle would have to wait for the big payment."

He went on, "The payments they were making were not enough and they would not discuss timing on the large payment. My uncle went ballistic. He had the foreclosure notices drafted. I just delivered them rather than have a stranger do it for a service fee."

Megan put her hand to her forehead and tried to work over the problem in her mind. "What can we do?"

"I attempted to tell your father that I would try and sell the home and make them whole to the extent we get enough on a sale," Ryan said. "He would potentially not have lost any money that he'd invested. I'd talked my uncle into it."

Ryan continued, "I couldn't talk to your father about it because he kicked me out. He obviously refused to read the letter that explained it. Under the circumstances, I can't imagine anyone being more fair. We had no choice but to foreclose." Ryan studied Megan. "I'll still work it out with your mom if she's interested in talking. I don't know why they wouldn't talk about it. I even had a great lender to work with them."

"That's probably because the restaurant is failing and they wouldn't qualify for a loan with anyone else," Megan said.

"The restaurant is failing?" Ryan looked surprised. "But it's a nice place and I've heard the food is great."

"Only to those who don't listen to bogus reviews and rumors." Megan clenched her hands. "Apparently there's a man with a vendetta against Mom and Dad and he's been creating a lot of problems. They can't prove it, but the signs are there."

Ryan narrowed his gaze. "Who is this guy?"

"Roger Meyer," she said. "He owns the restaurant next door to the Hummingbird Café."

"I know who he is." Ryan's frowned. "Why don't you tell me the story while I take Laredo into the barn?"

Megan nodded her agreement and she fell into step beside

him as he took the horse's reins and they headed for the barn. The horse's hooves clopped on the ground and its glossy coat gleamed in the late afternoon light.

She relayed what her parents had told her about Meyer, including the fact that he'd wanted to lease the building to expand his own restaurant. Her parents had outbid him and Meyer had told them they'd be sorry they ever opened it.

"Where's Ossie?" she asked as they walked.

"In the barn with Bill, one of my part-timers," Ryan said. As she walked by him she caught his scent of sun-warmed flesh, horse, and leather.

He paused and caught her by her hand. "I missed you, Meg."

She swallowed then said, "I missed you, too."

He smiled and they stepped into the barn. She sneezed from the dust wafting through the air from the alfalfa hay. A young man was taking hay bales off of the bed of a truck and stacking them in a corner of the barn. The dust from the bales floated in the air.

"Bill," Ryan said and the young man looked up from what he was doing. He took off his work gloves, tucked them into his back pocket, and walked toward Ryan and Megan.

"Bill, this is Megan." He turned to Megan. "This is Bill, one of my ranch hands."

The young man hurried to take off his green John Deere cap and shook Megan's hand. His grip was firm, his palm callused. "Nice to meet you, ma'am," he said.

"Good to meet you too, Bill," she said.

"How's your mama?" Ryan asked Bill with a concerned expression.

Bill shook his head. "Not so good."

"Does she need any more help?" Ryan asked.

"That check you gave us was more than enough, sir." Bill shook his head. "It helped get us through this month. Now that you got that part-time job for me with Miss Danica, I should make enough for us to pay our bills."

"What about the medical expenses?" Ryan asked, his eyes intense.

Bill stared at the ground then met Ryan's gaze. "I don't know how we're going to pay them. We'll just pray. It's about all that we can do."

Ryan put his hand on Bill's shoulder. "We'll figure something out."

Bill looked earnest. "You've done more than enough."

Ryan handed the horse's reins to Bill. "Put up Laredo for me after you brush her down."

"Yes, sir." Bill gripped the reins, said good day to Megan, then took the horse down the aisle between the stalls and disappeared into the back of the barn.

She turned from watching Bill leave and saw that Ryan was putting on a green work shirt. She was both relieved not to have the distraction of his naked chest and disappointed because she missed the view.

But then reality hit her and the pain of her father's death caused her to choke up and tears blurred her eyes.

Ryan seemed to realize what she was going through. He put his arm around her shoulders and guided her out of the barn and up to the house. She leaned her head against him as they walked. Her anger had faded but the pain felt magnified.

They went into his house and he got out a jar of sun tea and poured each of them a glass and added ice. He took a long drink of his tea, clearly needing something after being out working in the sun. She sipped hers and it soothed her a little.

She stared at her glass as they stood by the counter. "My mom isn't doing very well and we haven't been able to open the restaurant since my father died."

When she looked at Ryan she saw that he was watching her. "We'll figure something out," he said. "There's got to be a solution, we just need to find it."

She nodded. "I hope you're right." She paused. "I saw you in the church and at the cemetery. Thank you for coming to my father's funeral."

"I wanted to pay my respects," he said. "I care about you and how you were hurting for someone you loved. I just wanted to be there whether you knew it or not."

"I'm sorry I didn't answer or return your calls," she said.

"You just went through a lot, Meg." He studied her. "I don't blame you for anything."

She set her glass down on the counter. "Thank you."

He placed his glass beside hers and took her by her shoulders. "Tell me that your feelings for me haven't changed."

Memories of everything they'd done together flipped through her mind...from the county fair, to their dinner out, to dancing, camping... They'd packed a lot into the short time they'd known each other.

And during that time she'd seen how much people liked him, how kind he was, how thoughtful. A lot made up the man, and she knew that she could never stop loving him.

"I should have given you the chance to explain." She met his gaze. "I hope you can forgive me."

"There's nothing to forgive." He bent closer and kissed her forehead, then stroked hair from her face. His hand felt warm as it skimmed her cheek. "Let me know if you need anything, all right?"

"Okay." She gave a slow nod. "Thank you."

"You don't need to thank me." He hooked his finger beneath her chin and raised her head. "I would do anything for you. Anything."

"Your support means a lot to me." She brushed the tear from her eye that came from nowhere. His sincerity, his caring, meant the world to her.

He wrapped his arms around her in a tight embrace, catching her off guard. The next thing she knew, she was crying on his shoulder.

"Cry all you need to, honey." He rocked her as she sobbed, the weight of her father's death crumbling down on her.

He was gone. Her father was gone.

But he'd given her a gift when he'd told her he was proud of her, and all of the other things he said that she would hold in her heart forever.

"Do you have time for dinner?" Ryan asked. "I can fix something here or we can go out."

Drying her tears with her fingertips, she drew away from Ryan. "It's getting late. I should probably get home. My mom still isn't doing well."

He put his arm around her shoulders and walked out into the dusk to his truck and took her to the passenger side. Before he let her climb into it, he gave her a kiss that soothed her and sent warmth throughout her.

On the drive back to town, he held her hand on the console. The connection between them felt vibrant and alive.

While he drove in the darkness, he asked her about the restaurant and how business had been.

"Tess could tell you more than I can," Megan said. "She's been working with my parents in their restaurants since she was a teenager." Megan gave a self-deprecating smile. "I've never had the aptitude for it. I made a terrible waitress, I can't cook, and running a restaurant takes a special set of skills."

Ryan nodded but looked thoughtful. "I've never run a restaurant, but I'm a businessman and I may have some ideas for you. Let me think on it."

"Any ideas you might have would be welcome," Megan said.

When they reached her parents' home, he parked and walked around to her side of the truck and helped her out. He cupped her face as he looked down at her, a streetlight illuminating her face.

"I've missed you," he told her again as his gaze searched hers. "Please don't leave me again."

"I've missed you, too." Her voice came out softly.

He lowered his head and brought his lips to hers. It was a searching kiss, a loving kiss that permeated every bone in her body. She felt it flow through her like warm rain on a summer's day.

When he drew away from the kiss, she smiled up at him. He looked like he wanted to say something else but he just studied her as if holding tight onto whatever it was that he was thinking.

She smiled up at him and gave him one last look before she walked up the stairs, into her home.

CHAPTER 20

Still feeling the warmth of Ryan's kiss, Megan dreamily walked
up the stairs to the porch of her parents' home. She glanced over
her shoulder and smiled as he waved to her then pulled his truck
away from the curb. She stayed there, watching and waiting until
his red taillights disappeared into the night.

For a long moment she stood on the porch, daydreaming
about him. She wrapped her arms around a column, her head resting against the wood as she looked out on the street of the dark,
tree-shaded neighborhood.

He'd said there was nothing to forgive after the way she had
ignored his calls and messages. He'd understood what she was going through and the doubts that had been in her mind.

No doubt the first day she'd met him was the day that she'd

fallen in love with him. Everything she'd seen of him and had experienced with him since then had made her feelings grow stronger day by day.

The time she'd been separated from him had been excruciatingly painful. It had been as if a part of her had been torn away and her heart ripped to shreds. She'd never felt anything like that for any other man. Not even close. She'd locked the pain deep inside of her but he'd given her the key to unlock the pain and release it.

While they'd been camping, he'd said he thought he was falling for her. Did he still feel that way? Everything he'd done and said made her feel as though that hadn't changed. She'd certainly fallen for him and hard. He was a good man and she was blessed to have him in her life.

Should she have told him how she felt? No, not yet. She'd wait until the time was right.

She moved away from the column to the front door. She grasped the doorknob, let herself into her parents' home, and closed the door behind her.

"You ungrateful child." Margaret's shriek jerked Megan from her thoughts of Ryan.

Margaret was standing by the window, the curtain pulled partly back. She'd seen the kiss.

Heat flooded through Megan as she tried to talk over her mother's screaming. "Mom, let me explain—"

"How could you?" Margaret yelled. "After what that man did to our family, to your father. He killed your father!"

"Mom." Megan put strength behind her words. "Calm down. There are some things we need to discuss."

Margaret moved toward Megan. "There's nothing you can say

that will excuse what you have done." Margaret's hand flew up and she slapped Megan.

With shock, Megan stared at her mother. She brought her fingers to her stinging cheek, unable to believe her mother had just slapped her.

Margaret raised her hand again, but Megan grabbed her mother's wrist. Margaret tried to jerk away, but Megan held on.

Anger rose in Megan but she maintained her calm. Margaret's husband had just died and she blamed it on Ryan. But her mother had no right to treat Megan that way, no matter what she was going through.

"Sit down, Mom." Steel was in Megan's voice. So many times she hadn't defended herself just to avoid making waves. Not anymore. "It's time you listened to me."

"I'll do nothing of the kind." Margaret snarled the words.

"*Sit.*" Megan pointed to the couch beside Margaret. "I need to tell you what Dad said to me before he died."

It was as if Margaret's legs gave out on her and she sat on the edge of the couch. "What did your father say?"

"Among other things, Dad said that my judgment is sound and that I need to trust it." Megan took a step closer to where her mother was sitting. "In my judgment, Ryan McBride is a good man. Over the time that I've known him, I've seen the person that he is and I like what I see."

Megan went on, "I've seen how much people like him, from children to adults, and how much he cares. I've seen how kind he is, giving money to a mother who has cancer and her son. He is a good man, Mom."

"How can you say that?" Margaret curled her hands into fists on her lap. "He killed your father."

"No, he didn't." Megan put her hands on her hips. "Ryan was the messenger. He doesn't even own the house. He was helping his uncle."

Margaret opened her mouth as if to say something else.

"I'm not finished." Megan held up her hand. "Ryan tried to be the go-between to work things out, but Dad wouldn't even hear him out. Ryan gave Dad suggestions and attempted to make it work between you two and his uncle."

Margaret narrowed her gaze. "What suggestions?"

Megan went through the ideas that Ryan had proposed. "Selling the house is probably the best solution for all parties," Megan added. "It would be enough to pay off the balloon payment and give you back the money you invested. You would be able to buy another house that cost less."

"But this is where your father and I lived together." Margaret's lips started to tremble and then her face seemed to crumple. She buried her face in her hands. Her shoulders shook and sobs wracked her body.

Megan's gut twisted as she sat beside her mother and put an arm around her shoulders. She stroked her mother's hair as she cried.

Margaret raised her head, tears streaming down her face. "I don't know what to do. I lost your father... I'm losing this house... the restaurant is going." She looked so sad that Megan's heart ached. "My whole world is collapsing," Margaret sobbed.

Megan hugged her mother tighter, trying to think of the right words to say. "We'll think of something, Mom. It will work out."

Margaret looked through her tears at her fisted hands in her lap. She slowly relaxed them so that they weren't clenched anymore. She met Megan's eyes. "I'm sorry I slapped you. Can you forgive me?"

"Of course, Mom. You're having a hard time with Dad's passing and it's only been two days since the funeral, and everything else," Megan said. "I understand that."

Margaret hugged Megan, holding on to her like a lifeline.

CHAPTER 21

Ryan drove along the street, his thoughts filled with Megan. She was a special woman and after finding her, he didn't intend to let her go.

It was poker night in the back room of the Highlander bar and Ryan's cousin, Jack Parks, had invited Ryan to sit in on the game in the past. Maybe they had an extra chair at the table tonight.

As he drove, he dialed his cousin's number from the phone's address book and waited for him to pick up.

"How's it going?" Jack answered.

"It's getting better." Ryan put on his turn signal as he came up to a corner. "Are you playing poker at the Highlander tonight?"

"As long as Carrie doesn't keep me home I'll be leaving soon," Jack said. "Why, you want to join us tonight?"

"I'm in town." Ryan drummed his fingers on the steering wheel. "Thought I'd stop at the Highlander and have a beer, and remembered it's poker night."

"George Johnson hasn't been showing up lately," Jack said. "I think there'll be room for one more."

"I'll be there." Ryan disconnected the call and headed for the bar.

The Highlander was a down and dirty bar in the older part of Prescott. Ryan parked a few spaces down from the bar then headed inside.

Inside, the air was thick with smoke and a little hazy. The crack of billiards came from two tables in the corner along with the whump of darts hitting the target on his left. On his right was a mechanical bull. Ryan's brother Creed, a world champion bull rider, was one of the few who could take the metal beast at its highest setting.

The bar proudly sported a couple of autographed pictures of Creed, their hometown hero, on one of his most famous rides. The framed pictures in black and white hung on the wall by the bull. Pictures of other popular rodeo performers also covered the walls in the same area. Creed was a modest and good-natured cowboy who took fame in stride.

Ryan went up to the bar and ordered a Rolling Rock.

A couple of Ryan's old buddies were shooting pool so he dropped cash on the bar, grabbed his beer, and sauntered over to where they were playing. Duke Carter and Joel Ellison greeted him with slaps to the back and invited him to find a partner and play doubles, but Ryan declined.

They shot the bull for a while before Ryan spotted Jack coming in through the front entrance of the bar. He told Duke and Joel he'd see them around and then headed over to Jack.

"Damn but I could use a beer," Jack said as they reached the bar.

"Let me buy you a cold one." Ryan set his empty on the polished wood surface. "Tough day at work?"

Jack gave a wry smile. "Something like that."

Ryan ordered another Rolling Rock and Jack asked for a Bud. After Ryan paid for their beers, he followed Jack through a doorway in the back and into a dark-paneled hallway. To the right was the kitchen and in the opposite direction was a back room. They headed down the hallway toward it.

The moment Jack opened the door the smell of cigar smoke met Ryan. A wood-bladed fan turned lazily overhead, stirring the smoke and offering a brush of cool air. The room was also paneled in dark wood and the old wood furniture was scuffed and scarred. A large round table was at the center of the room, a smaller table stood to the side with poker chips piled on it along with a box to hold the cash the players used to buy chips.

Inside the room, four men stood or sat at the round table, two of them puffing on cigars, all of them with drinks in their hands. Poker chips were piled in front of each man. Ryan recognized two of the men, including Roger Meyer, who was standing.

"Gentlemen, if you don't already know him, this is Ryan McBride." Jack jerked his thumb toward Ryan. "If we've got an extra seat at the table, Ryan here would like to join in on the fun. George hasn't been able to make it for a while, so I thought I'd bring in another sap to lose some money at our table."

The men chuckled and Ryan laughed good-naturedly. Roger

Meyer clapped his hand on the shoulder of the dark-haired man that he was standing behind. "This here is Julian Taylor who's also new and here to lose his shirt to me."

Jack went around the table introducing everyone else for the benefit of both Taylor and Ryan—Henry Rodriguez, Roger Meyer, and David Danbury. Danbury mentioned that he was a reporter for the Prescott Review. Taylor didn't volunteer any information, seeming to keep to himself and being fairly quiet.

"Even if George makes it, we'll have room for McBride." Meyer indicated the chair next to him. "I could use a little extra cash tonight." He looked friendly enough, but there was an edge to him that Ryan didn't trust.

Ryan took the seat beside Meyer who gripped a glass of amber liquid in his hand.

"What are you drinking?" Ryan gestured to Meyer's drink.

Meyer raised the glass. "Whiskey, straight."

Rodriguez took Ryan's cash and pushed stacks of poker chips in front of him.

Sophie, a dark-haired waitress in a low-cut white blouse and tiny black skirt entered the room. Ryan ordered a whiskey on the rocks. Roger ordered a bottle of Jack Daniels.

He didn't know Meyer well, but had heard things about the man over the years. He was considered a ladies' man yet there were rumors that he treated his women poorly. Ryan had been told of business dealings with him that had gone south and Meyer had the reputation of being a tough S.O.B to work with.

When the waitress returned, Jack was just pulling his chair up to the table and Rodriguez was shuffling the deck. Sophie set the bottle of whiskey in front of Meyer before giving Ryan his drink.

She leaned over so that he got a clear view of her cleavage. Ryan started a tab and when he ignored her show of breasts, she pouted and left the room.

Ryan picked up his glass of whiskey and watched as Meyer filled his own glass from the bottle. Meyer asked if anyone else was up for some whiskey. Danbury and Rodriguez accepted the offer and Ryan said he'd take a hit once he'd finished his drink. Jack and Julian declined. Jack couldn't risk going home stinking drunk because Carrie would kill him, so he stuck with a max of four beers a night. Jack did accept a cigar from Rodriguez.

When Rodriguez finished dealing, Ryan picked up his cards and studied them. He had a good hand to start with and he matched Meyer's bids. Ryan called and Meyer had three of a kind, which beat Ryan's two pair.

As they played, Meyer kept filling his own glass and kept topping off Ryan's. Ryan nursed his drink slowly because he didn't plan on drinking much. He'd be driving home tonight and he wasn't about to drive drunk. However, Meyer didn't have the same reservations and it wasn't long before the man really loosened up.

Ryan asked Meyer about the man's restaurant, the Chuck Wagon. Meyer loved to talk about his place and claimed that it was one of the best steakhouses in the west.

"A new restaurant is next to your place." Ryan said between hands.

"That shithole?" Meyer gave a laugh. "You wouldn't want to go there."

Ryan felt a little heat at his collar. He took a swig of his whiskey then set the glass down. "I heard you wanted to expand your restaurant into that place but the Dysons outbid you on the deal."

The man's face darkened. "And I'm making sure they regret it."

Ryan gave a conspiratorial laugh as he tried to stay relaxed while he poured Meyer more whiskey. "How are you managing that?"

Meyer grinned and slurred, "I have my ways."

"Sounds like you're making sure they don't get away with taking property that was rightfully yours," Ryan said. If the man was out to hurt the Dysons, Ryan wanted to know about it. "Think you can get the place if they end up being shut down?"

"That's the plan." Meyer knocked back the rest of his whiskey. He slammed the glass down on the table and seemed to wobble in his seat. "A few complaints lodged with the Health Department, reports on employing illegal immigrants, some bad reviews—won't be long now. Maybe a few people will get sick there."

Meyer elbowed his cousin, the reporter, David Danbury. "I think it's time for another review in a few days."

Danbury grinned. "Whenever you want it, just let me know."

Meyer slapped him on the back. "Place is closed temporarily because the old man kicked it. When they try to open it again, we'll let 'em have it and sink their ship. This time we'll really make it count."

"Are you talking about reviews?" Ryan asked, barely reining in his anger.

Meyer snorted. "Reviews will only go so far. I've got something else in mind. I'm not done yet and I won't be done until I take over that location."

The man leaned back in his chair and continued, "I'll expand and that side will be a bar and I'll leave the restaurant as is. I'll have nightly entertainment, dancing, and a fully stocked bar that'll be a hell of a lot better than this dump. Might even move our weekly poker game over there."

Ryan nodded, smiling, when what he wanted to do was kick the sonofabitch's ass. But for now he needed to get any info he could out of Meyer and he wasn't going to do it with the man at the end of Ryan's boot.

Jack started dealing and they returned to the game. Ryan won a few hands but lost more than he won, but considering these guys had been playing together for some time, he didn't think he was doing too badly.

In between hands, Ryan tried to strike up a conversation with Meyer again, but the man had moved on to other subjects to rant about and Ryan didn't want his questions to come off as suspicious if he pressed on about the café.

So the bastard had plans once the café was re-opened. Somehow Ryan needed to head it off. But what the hell could he do if he didn't even know what the man was up to?

Ryan wanted to confront Meyer, but he needed to process what he'd heard and talk with Megan.

Her parents hadn't been exaggerating when they'd told Megan that Meyer had it in for them.

Now what could they do about it?

CHAPTER 22

Over the next week, Megan helped Margaret and Tess prepare to reopen the Hummingbird Café. Margaret and Tess interviewed a couple of cooks to replace Paul and hired Julian Taylor who had been the cook at the Prancing Pony before it had gone out of business several months earlier, thanks to the economy.

Early on re-opening day, a Friday, Megan accompanied her mother and sister to the restaurant. Normally, the restaurant was open for lunch and dinner, but for re-opening day they would be opening at five for dinner.

Megan had designed a quarter-page advertisement for the Hummingbird Café with a "buy one dinner get one free" coupon, which they had put in the paper as a grand re-opening special. Megan had suggested it as a way for people to know the restaurant was open again and to draw people in. They hoped for a good-sized dinner crowd.

They drove in two separate cars to the restaurant, and reached it at the same time. Their parking lot was next to the convenience store and they had a view of the side of the store. Megan didn't really like the restaurant being located so close to a gas station, but from what her parents had said, the rent was good and they did get some lunch traffic from customers of the gas station.

Margaret frowned when they went to the back door. "Someone broke in," Margaret said as she looked at Tess and Megan.

"What?" Tess's voice raised an octave as her eyes widened.

Margaret stepped back to show Tess and Megan that the doorknob was loose and the door itself was opened a crack.

Tess moved in front of her mother and pushed the door open. The door creaked as sunlight spilled across the immaculate kitchen. "Nothing looks disturbed," Tess said, her mouth turned down into a frown.

"Did you leave cash in the register?" Megan asked as she followed the other two into the restaurant.

Tess shook her head. "I always clean it out at night and put the money into the safe. When I closed up the restaurant two weeks ago, I left a minimal amount of cash in the safe and took the rest to the bank."

"We'd better check the safe," Megan said.

Tess led the way to the wall safe that was in the office behind a file cabinet. They pulled the cabinet away from the wall. "It doesn't look touched." She knelt in front of it and put in the code. The safe made a *thunking* sound and then the door swung open. Tess drew out the moneybag and flipped through the cash in it. "Everything is here," she said before locking the safe again. She left out the bag in order to put the cash into the register when they opened for dinner.

The three of them switched on the lights and searched the restaurant for anything out of place or missing, but came across nothing.

"Not worth calling the police since nothing seems touched or missing," Tess said.

"Maybe it was kids," Megan said. "They could have been scared off before they had a chance to come in and wreak any havoc."

Tess nodded. "That could be it."

Margaret didn't say anything. She looked sad and as if she was having a hard time being there. It was the first time she'd been in the restaurant since her husband had passed away.

Megan swallowed. It wasn't easy for her to be here, either. She remembered the last time she'd seen her father in the kitchen and how he had been hard at work at the stove. He'd been stirring chili and she could almost smell it now. The memory caused an ache behind Megan's eyes. It was difficult enough for her to be here right now and she couldn't imagine how her mother was feeling.

They opened up the doors and windows, allowing the cool breeze to freshen everything up. The café had been closed for two weeks and it was stuffy inside. The restaurant needed to be open and ready for dinnertime, with a good crowd to serve, hopefully. After being closed for more than a week, they weren't anticipating much of a crowd until people got used to the place being open again, but hopefully the ad would make a difference.

The new cook, who was to replace Paul, showed up around

noon to prep for dinner. Julian seemed nice enough as he got to work, although he was on the quiet side. He gave Megan an odd feeling—probably due to the fact that he kept to himself. But then again, her father had been quiet and focused when he worked in the kitchen, too.

Fortunately, the young man Tucker, who served as both busboy and dishwasher, hadn't gone on to find other employment during the past two weeks and was still with them.

Megan worked on things that didn't involve running the café itself—Tess and Margaret took care of all of that. Megan went to the flower shop on the other side of the convenience store and bought red carnations while she arranged for the morning flower delivery to start once again. She returned to the restaurant and cleaned the clear glass vases, filled them with water, and put fresh cut carnations in each one before setting a vase on each table. She cleaned the front window and it sparkled as sunlight came in through the window, casting a dazzling radiance on the place.

She helped Tess make sure the bathrooms were cleaned, sprayed air freshener to freshen the atmosphere and then dusted and cleaned off every surface in the café, including mopping the floor.

They filled the condiment containers to be ready for guests, and cleaned and refilled the glass salt and pepper shakers, and put them on the tables. Silverware wrapped in cloth napkins was put on each table. Tess and Megan went over everything twice just to make sure it was all done.

Tucker showed up in the afternoon and they put him to work, too. He was a nice kid, about eighteen, and a hard worker who finished his jobs quickly and efficiently then asked what else he could do to help.

Megan had designed new menus during the week using her talents as a graphic designer and they made sure the specials were with each menu. Today the special was chicken pasta parmesan, something that Julian had said was a specialty of his, and he prepped the ingredients for the dish.

The dessert of the day was Margaret's peach pie. They had a couple of other desserts, but she was already known for her pies. As far as duties, Margaret would go wherever she was needed. She would cook, serve, or do anything else that needed to be done.

The sun was setting as the time rolled around for the café to open for dinner. The lights had been dimmed slightly and the clear bud vases and drinking glasses on the tables sparkled.

Megan played hostess—waitressing skills were beyond her talents. She'd worn a simple black dress that complemented her figure and fairly sensible but pretty low heels that went well with the dress. She'd pulled her hair back into an elegant knot.

She greeted the first guests, showed them to a table, and gave them each a menu after they sat down. She told them the specials before returning to the hostess station.

The restaurant filled with the rich smells of food as people ordered dinner. The chicken pasta parmesan was a big hit and a goodly number of patrons chose the dish as their entrée.

Ryan showed up and gave Megan a kiss as he reached the hostess station.

Her face warmed. "There are people around."

He grinned. "And now they'll know you belong to me."

His words sent heat through her. He was staking a claim on her and she loved it.

She escorted him to a table and their eyes lingered on each other. He brushed her hand with his fingertips as he took the menu from her.

Pretty soon it became apparent that Ryan had something to do with the crowd now in the café. His brothers and cousins and a good many of his friends and their spouses or dates showed up. The town was apparently filled with McBrides.

The night flew by, people complimenting the food and the service. The place was much busier than expected and Megan did what she could in between manning the hostess station. She refilled glasses with water and iced tea.

"If this keeps up, we're going to need to hire another server," Tess said with a sparkle in her eyes. "I've never seen this place so busy."

"I think Ryan had something to do with that." Megan gave a nod in the direction of his table where several of his friends were now sitting. "His relatives and friends are packing the place."

"From what I've seen of him and from what you've told me, he really is a good guy." Tess smiled. "I'd say he's a keeper."

"Yeah, he is." Megan returned her sister's smile. "How's Mom doing?"

"She's been as happy as can be expected without Dad. She thinks Julian is a fairly good cook, but is keeping an eye on him. You know how Mom is. He could be fabulous and she would say he was competent."

"Yes, I certainly do know how she is." Megan nodded. "People seemed happy enough with the food."

By the time closing rolled around, Megan was dead on her feet. She locked the door after the final customer left and turned over the "Closed" sign.

She turned to Tess. "If this keeps up, you may have to hire two more servers for the weekends while you hostess." Megan rolled her shoulders and stretched. "I can't take much more time from my graphic design business. I have work piling high."

"Thank you for being here for us to get this place going again." Tess hugged her. "The idea for the advertisement and coupon was genius. Dad would have been so happy to see the café full like it was tonight."

"It was fantastic." Megan held back a yawn. "How were tips?"

Tess put her hands in her apron pocket and took out a thick wad of cash. "Tips were great. I'll be sharing them with you and Tucker."

Megan shook her head. "Set my cut aside for Jenny." She narrowed her eyes at Tess when it looked like her sister was going to protest. "One way or another it goes to my adorable niece. Put it into her college fund."

Megan looked over her shoulder at Ryan who approached her. She glanced back at Tess. "Does Mom know we have Ryan to thank for a lot of our full house?"

"I made sure she does," Tess said with a nod.

When Ryan reached them, Tess surprised all of them by hugging him. "Thank you," she said as she stepped back. "You really made a difference tonight."

"The great service and food are what sold people on the place," he said. "You deserved it."

"Come on." Tess gave a nod toward the kitchen. "I think Mom wants to talk to you, Ryan."

Megan cut a look at Tess but her sister was smiling. If Tess wasn't worried about her mother's reaction, then Megan figured she shouldn't be, either.

"What started out with a break-in has turned out to be a fantastic day," Tess said to Megan.

Ryan frowned. "There was a break-in?"

Megan nodded. "We couldn't find anything missing or disturbed. I almost forgot about it."

Ryan followed Tess and Megan to the kitchen where Tucker was washing pots and pans and Julian was cleaning up the stove. Ryan went up to the cook who seemed surprised to see him.

"We met at the poker game last week." Ryan held out his hand. "Julian Taylor, am I right?"

The man took Ryan's hand but didn't smile. "You're McBride," he said before releasing Ryan's hand and turning back to his work.

"That was odd," Megan said quietly to Tess. "He sure wasn't very friendly to Ryan."

When Margaret saw Ryan she paused. It was difficult to read her expression. She walked toward them and studied him for a moment.

"I'm sorry I misjudged you," she said. "And I want to thank you for tonight."

"Anything I can do to help, let me know." He started rolling up his sleeves. "Including anything that needs to be cleaned up and readied for tomorrow."

Margaret smiled and looked at Megan. "Where did you find him?"

Megan laughed.

When the place was cleaned and everything was done in preparation for the following day, everyone headed home. After

Tess locked up and they'd walked her to her car, Ryan and Megan stood by his truck.

They stood outside in the quiet, cool night. Stars glittered in the sky and the breeze caused goose bumps to rise on her skin.

"Why don't you come to my house tonight?" he asked as he settled his hands at her waist.

"I'm not sure I'd be much fun." She moved her hands up his chest and gripped his collar. "I'm so tired that all I'm good for is a long hot bath and some nice clean sheets."

"I'd be happy to wash your back." He lowered his mouth to hers. "I'd love to wash you anywhere you want."

When his lips met hers fire burned through her. She felt a renewed energy that came out of nowhere.

When he drew away, she smiled up at him, looking into his gorgeous eyes. "I think I just got my second wind."

CHAPTER 23

Ryan and Megan drove to her parents' home so that she could drop off her car and get a few things. He waited outside for her in the cool night, watching the stars. Before she walked into the house, a shooting star blazed across the sky.

"A good omen," she said as she smiled up at him and he gave her a light kiss before she went inside the house.

While she was in the house, she grabbed a bottle of bubble bath and stuck it in her duffel. Who knew if cowboys had bubble bath?

"Goodnight, Mom." She hugged her mom when she emerged back into the living room.

"Thank you for everything, Megan." Margaret looked at her daughter. "Your father would have been so proud of you both tonight."

"He would have been proud of all of us." Megan kissed her mother's cheek before going to the front door. She gave her mother a little wave before heading out the door.

Outside, Ryan leaned up against his truck, his hands in his pockets as he waited for her. He looked so good standing there, his body large and muscular, moonlight and his western hat shading his face.

He kissed her and took her duffel before helping her into his truck. Once they were in his vehicle and he was driving, she relaxed against the seat, her body hurting everywhere possible. Even her hair and her teeth seemed to ache.

"I haven't been this tired in longer than I can remember." She looked at Ryan as she melted into the seat. "I'm going to land face first in your bed after I take a bath."

"Then I'll slide into bed and cuddle you," he said with a smile.

He was so sweet that she had to smile back at him. "Cuddling sounds good."

The thirty-minute drive to his ranch went by quickly as they talked about the success of the evening. The truck vibrated over the cattle guard as they went through the gates and then he pulled the truck up to the house. As tired as Megan was, it was nice to have him come around the truck and help her climb out.

Ossie greeted them, bounding around and running back and forth from Megan and Ryan to the house and back, as if welcoming them and telling them it was time to go in.

Megan's feet felt heavy as they climbed up the steps to the front door and she leaned on his shoulder.

"Bath," she said as soon as they walked in and she kicked off her low heels. "I desperately need that bath."

He smiled. "And a bath you are going to get."

Ossie looked up hopefully, as if she wanted to accompany them and climb into the tub, too.

"Not you, girl." Ryan grinned and ruffled the hair on Ossie's head. "Stay here."

Ossie lowered herself to the floor and put her head on her paws as she looked up at them with her big blue eyes.

Ryan took Megan by her hand and led her into the master bedroom where he removed his boots and socks.

In the master bath he had a tub big enough for two. He started the water, running it until it was warm before he began to fill up the tub. She took her orange blossom-scented bubble bath from her duffel and poured a goodly amount into the water. Immediately, mounds of bubbles started growing in the tub.

While the tub filled, he took her by the shoulders, turned her around, and slowly unzipped her dress. He let it slide from her shoulders, over her breasts, and along her hips until it slipped to the floor.

With her back still to him, he kissed her nape as he unfastened her bra and let it fall on top of the dress.

"I love you just like this." He pressed his body against her almost naked form as he ran his hands along her shoulders and down her arms and up again. His clothing felt rough brushing her back, his cock rigid against her ass. Despite her exhaustion, she found desire stirring inside her.

"No fair." She gave a soft moan. "You aren't supposed to seduce me."

"Mmmm…" He kissed one side of her neck and moved his

lips behind her ear. She shivered as he moved his mouth to the other ear, his breath warm on her skin. He took the clip out of her hair and let the mass swing down to her shoulders.

"I love your body," he murmured as he slipped his fingers into the waistband of her panties. "I love to see you and touch you."

He lowered himself on one knee and then pushed her panties down to her ankles. She stepped out of them and he eased to his feet again, moving his hands along her calves to her thighs and lingering on her ass and hips. His palms were warm wherever he touched her yet she shivered as if cold.

Desire swirled inside her. It was so much more than want and need… like she had to have him more than anything she'd ever needed before in her life. She ached between her thighs and her heart beat faster.

Her belly fluttered as his fingertips trailed along her waist to the sides of her breasts. He lightly skimmed his fingers over her breasts then palmed them both as he pressed himself against her.

She swallowed as she looked at the steam rising from the tub. "The water. It's getting pretty high."

He gave a low laugh then leaned down to turn off the water before returning to his position behind Megan.

His body felt warm against hers and she looked over her shoulder. Her voice was husky as she said, "Take off your clothes."

She turned to face him as he reached for the top button of his western shirt. Impatiently, she moved his hands away and unbuttoned it for him, letting her fingers brush against the hard muscles beneath. She kissed his throat, his masculine scent inviting her to run her tongue over each of his flat male nipples. She pushed his shirt over his shoulders and down his arms and they let it fall onto her dress.

He sucked in his breath as she licked a path from his chest, down his abs to the waistband of his jeans. She knelt and undid his belt buckle then unbuttoned his jeans. She drew down the zipper, exposing his boxer briefs.

She pushed his jeans over his hips and down until he kicked them aside. His underwear outlined his erection and she skimmed her fingers along the hard ridge. She slid her fingers into the waistband and pulled at the cloth, drawing it to the floor before she tossed them somewhere in the bathroom when he stepped out of them.

The skin of his cock was so soft over the steel of his erection and she breathed in his masculine scent. She darted her tongue out and tasted the bead of semen on the head and he sucked in his breath.

"I promised you a bath." He grasped her shoulders and drew her to her feet. "And that's what I'm going to give you before all of these bubbles are gone."

She smiled and he leaned down and kissed her, a soft delicious kiss that somehow renewed her. He helped her into the tub and she sank into the water and slid beneath the bubbles and gave a soft moan of pleasure. She closed her eyes and smiled as the exquisite feeling of a warm bath relaxed her.

Water splashed over the side and onto the tile as Ryan joined her. She opened one eye and saw his smile as he sat on the opposite side of the tub and put his legs to either side of hers. The faucet was on the side of the tub between them, so it wasn't in the way. They could both relax and enjoy the wonderful warm water.

He crooked his finger. "Come here."

She raised her eyebrows, but when he motioned to her again she obeyed, scooting closer to him, bubbles clinging to her body.

"Turn around and sit between my thighs," he said.

"What do you have in mind?" she asked him.

He raised a wet hand and pushed hair behind her ear, leaving a wet trail along her jaw. "Just turn around."

She did as he said and he adjusted her so that she was a few inches away from him. Then he picked up a cup that was on one corner of the tub beside a bottle of shampoo. He scooped up a cupful of water from the tub then poured the warm water over her hair.

The water felt good as it rushed over her scalp. He poured two more cups of water over her head until her hair was soaked. He poured an apple-scented shampoo into his palm and began working it into a lather in her hair.

She sighed as she relaxed into the feel of him massaging her scalp. When he was finished, he ran clean water from the faucet and let the warmth flow down her head, rinsing the shampoo away. The bubbles ran in rivulets over her breasts and into the bathwater.

After he'd washed away all of the shampoo, he picked up a washcloth from the counter beside the tub and wet it before pouring bath gel onto the cloth. He began by soaping her neck, moving the cloth over her shoulders and down her back.

He had her lean back into him so that she was resting her back against his chest and he could lean over her. He soaped her breasts and paused to play with her soap-slicked nipples, causing her to gasp with pleasure.

When he finished with her front, he adjusted her so that he could wash her legs and her tired feet as well.

As he took gentle care of her, she thought about what an in-credible man he was. She loved everything about him and couldn't help but want more of him every time they were together. His strong arms around her and the feel of his wet skin against hers as he soaped her body was heavenly.

"I feel so relaxed." She sighed. "I don't know if I can move again."

"The water is getting cool. Besides, I have plans for you." He moved aside her wet hair and kissed her ear. "Let's get you out of this tub."

"Do I have to get out? It feels great." She groaned, but good-naturedly.

"Yep." He moved her gently so that he could climb out of the tub. He took her hand and helped her step onto the rug beside the tub. The bathroom was no longer steamy since the water had cooled.

He grabbed a thick towel and rubbed her with it, drying her soft skin. He toweled her hair then ran a comb through the strands. After he had dried himself off, he led her out of the bathroom to his bedroom.

Despite the exhaustion of the day, and the continued aches in her body, she felt desire continue to move within her. When they reached the bed, she faced him and linked her arms around his neck. He settled his hands on her waist and looked at her for a long moment before kissing her softly.

"Lie on the middle of the bed on your belly." He ran his finger along her lower lip. "I have something planned for you."

She remembered when he'd had her get on her hands and knees on the bunk in the camper and a thrill went through her.

She wondered if he had anything like that in mind.

"Go on. Lie down." He gently directed her to the bed where he pulled away the comforter and the sheet. "I'll be right back."

She settled herself on her belly, resting her head on her folded arms, her face turned to the side. She watched him return with a bottle of lotion.

He sat on the edge of the bed and squirted lotion onto his palm then set the bottle aside and spread the cool substance across her back and her shoulders. The lotion had a light pleasant scent. His callused fingers were warm as he started to massage her shoulders.

His firm touch sent ripples of pleasure through her. His massage was deep and sensual as he worked out the kinks and knots in her neck and back.

She found herself lulled into a state where she felt like she was floating on fluffy clouds high above. She drifted in and out of consciousness, relaxing completely into his touch.

When he stopped his massage, she sighed and didn't think she'd be able to move again. He switched off the light and slid into bed beside her before taking her in his arms and holding her close to his warm body.

Despite the rigidity of his erection against her, all he did was hold her as she drifted off into a deep sleep.

CHAPTER 24

Ryan woke before Megan did and left to take care of chores. He thought of her warm body in his bed and he got his work done in record time.

When he returned to the house he slid into bed beside her. Her lips were soft as he gently kissed her awake. When she smiled at him he slipped inside her and they greeted the morning with a passion that had him on fire.

After breakfast, he drove Megan back to Prescott so that she could help her mother and sister prepare for another day at the restaurant. Ryan figured he'd volunteer to do what he could. If tonight was anything like yesterday, they would need all of the help they could get.

When they reached the restaurant, Ryan parked and he and

Megan walked through the back door and into the kitchen.

Tess looked frantic and Margaret was in near hysterics.

Margaret wrung her hands, her voice high. "How could this have happened?"

Tess hurried to Megan. "Thank God you're here."

Concern was written on Megan's face. "What's wrong?"

"We've been getting calls all morning." Tess looked close to tears. "People are claiming they have food poisoning. All of the people who got sick ate the chicken parmesan."

Ryan frowned. He'd eaten a cowboy steak rather than the chicken.

Megan's jaw dropped. "Food poisoning?"

Tess nodded. "Nine calls already and we had at least twenty people order that dish."

"We're always so careful." Margaret's eyes were rimmed with red. "We use only the best and freshest meats. The chicken was delivered the day before yesterday. We took some of it home the night before the grand reopening, and had it for dinner, and none of us got sick. The chicken here at the restaurant was kept refrigerated and the refrigerator registers 36 degrees. It didn't sit out at all." She shook her head. "It makes no sense."

"What about the company you bought it from?" Megan asked.

Tess shook her head. "They haven't had one complaint yet."

Ryan stood beside Megan, his expression grim. "You're right. This doesn't make sense."

"We sanitize everything." Margaret looked panicked. "It's the first thing we train our employees to do. I went through it immediately with Julian when he started with us yesterday."

"Julian Taylor." Ryan turned the man's name over in his mind.

He'd been at the poker game. He'd been fairly quiet, but he'd been friendly enough with Meyer.

"Yes," Tess said. "Do you know him?"

Ryan nodded. "I met him last week at a poker game. I don't know much about the man. He keeps to himself."

"He does," Tess said. "You don't suppose he didn't keep his cooking utensils and cutlery clean…"

"I made sure everything was done correctly," Margaret said. "I'm positive that everything was absolutely as clean as could possibly be."

"Mom is obsessed with cleanliness," Tess said. "There's no way it could have been the utensils."

The kitchen phone rang and everyone looked at it.

"I'll get it." Tess had a look of trepidation as she went to answer the phone. She answered, "Hummingbird Café," in a voice that sounded positive and perky, at complete odds with the concern on her features.

She listened then said, "You have my apologies and we will give you a coupon for two free dinners." Her features grew more distressed as she held the phone to her ear. "I understand," she finally said. "Again, you have our apologies."

When she'd put the receiver back on its cradle, she turned to the others. "That was another customer and his wife, and both had the chicken. They've filed a complaint with the Health Department."

"What do we do?" Margaret continued wringing her hands. "This will spread through town like wildfire."

Ryan turned it over and over in his mind. Something wasn't right here, something that nagged at him.

A knock came at the back door and Tess opened it. Her face paled as she saw a balding man and a tall woman, both with clipboards.

"I'm Inspector Reginald McDonald with the Health Department." He indicated the woman next to him. "This is Inspector Janice Canton. We've received multiple reports about food poisoning from food served by your restaurant. We'd like to come in."

Tess stepped out of the way and let the inspectors in.

"We've met before." McDonald held out his hand to Margaret. "When we received a previous complaint."

"Which turned out to be bogus," Tess said.

"That is true," McDonald said as he gripped Margaret's hand. "But this is a more serious problem. We understand that several of your patrons ate a chicken dinner you served and became ill."

The woman, Inspector Canton, started her inspection as Johnson spoke.

"We've had calls this morning." Margaret's back was rigid as she drew her hand away from McDonald. "But I don't understand how. We adhere to all regulations and our own strict precautions."

"We're required to research this problem thoroughly, Mrs. Dyson." McDonald gave a nod toward the refrigerator. "Is that where the chicken is kept?"

"Yes." Margaret started toward the fridge.

McDonald held up his hand. "I'll take a look myself."

Margaret stepped back and let McDonald past.

As the inspectors went through the kitchen, Ryan settled his hand on Megan's shoulder. "Can you think of anything odd happening?"

Megan and her sister shook their heads. Margaret watched

the inspectors.

Another knock came at the door and Tess answered it again.

When she opened the door, Ryan saw that it was the reporter from the poker game.

"I'm David Danbury with the Prescott Review." He had a serious expression. "We've received reports that you've had multiple customers with cases of food poisoning from last night and that the Health Department has been notified. How is it that your restaurant managed to get so many people ill?"

Tess slammed the door in the reporter's face.

"The newspaper already knows?" Margaret burst into tears and buried her face in her hands.

Tess put her arm around her mother's shoulders, looking close to tears herself.

"Come on, Mom," Megan said. "Sit down and I'll make a cup of blackberry tea."

"Blackberry tea?" Margaret looked almost hysterical again. "How is that supposed to calm me?"

"Just have a seat." Tess guided Margaret to the kitchen table.

Megan went to a cabinet and drew out a box of flavored teas and put a kettle on to boil.

Margaret watched the inspectors comb through the kitchen. "What if they shut us down?"

Tess rubbed Margaret's shoulder. "Have faith, Mom. Everything will work out."

"How?" Margaret sobbed. "Explain to me how this is all going to be all right."

Megan laid her hand on her mother's. "One step at a time, Mom. We'll get through this and the restaurant will survive."

That same something that had been bothering Ryan earlier nagged at him but he couldn't put his finger on it. What was it? Was there some explanation that was eluding him?

Mentally, he shook his head. Likely it was just the fact that he wanted to believe there was some way to help the Dysons. This might be one mess he couldn't help them climb out of.

CHAPTER 25

Megan sank onto a seat in the nearly empty restaurant that evening, a feeling of heaviness weighing her down. Last night had been a full house, incredible in every sense of the word. Today it was like a graveyard.

News of the food poisoning had spread quickly throughout the city, thanks in great part to the reporter from the Prescott Review.

But a television station from Phoenix had also picked up the story. It might have been a slow news day, but a reporter had pounced on the fact that nineteen people were reported to have come down with an illness from a Prescott restaurant. Someone from the news station tried to contact the owners of the Hummingbird Café, but Tess told the reporter that they had no comment.

The Health Department inspectors found no violations upon inspection of the restaurant. If anything, it was in remarkable condition, clean and sanitary on all levels. Of course, they took the tainted chicken to be tested.

Because no violations were found, the Dysons were allowed to keep the restaurant open, but the damage was done. Between rumors that spread across town by word of mouth, to the reports by both newspaper and TV news, the café had experienced a devastating blow.

All day Margaret had been almost inconsolable. Megan believed her mother's breakdown was in part due to the fact that her husband and partner had died only two weeks prior.

Julian hadn't shown up, probably fearing blame for the chicken since he'd been the cook. Maybe he had been to blame… Although for the life of her, Megan couldn't figure out how.

Earlier in the day they'd had fresh chicken delivered. The loss from the damage of the tainted chicken had cost them more than they could afford to lose. If this continued, it would shut down the business.

Ryan walked into the café and Megan rose to meet him. She went straight into his arms, needing a hug. He'd had to go back to the ranch today to get some work done and she'd wished he could have been at her side the entire day. It was a selfish thought, but she felt so much better with him around.

"You okay?" he asked as they headed toward the kitchen with his arm around her shoulders and her arm resting at his waist.

"I don't know." She sighed. "All of this—it's just so hard."

"Have you thought of or come across anything that might

give you some clue as to how the chicken was tainted?" he asked.

Megan shook her head as they walked into the kitchen. "It's a mystery."

Ryan saw Megan's mother. "Hi, Margaret," he said. "How are you holding up?"

She shrugged. "About as well as anyone could, I suppose."

"Where's your cook?" he asked as he looked at Megan.

"He didn't show up." Megan brushed a strand of hair from her face. "We're guessing he saw the news reports and thought he might be blamed."

Tess walked into the kitchen and put her hand on her hip. "Who knows? Maybe he is."

Ryan frowned. Why hadn't Julian Taylor shown up? Did he have something to do with the tainted meat?

A thought went through him that caused hair to prickle on his arms. Taylor had been at that poker game and he knew Meyer.

And Meyer had made a statement... That statement was what had been bothering Ryan—he just hadn't realized what it was that had been nagging him until now.

"Maybe a few people will get sick there."

That was what Meyer had said.

Had Meyer somehow sabotaged the chicken?

How? Through Taylor?

"Is something wrong?" Megan's voice brought Ryan out of his thoughts.

He shook his head. "Just have a few things on my mind." He offered her a smile. "It's nothing important." He wasn't ready to tell her his suspicions. He needed to figure out a few things.

"I've been thinking." Megan looked at the back door that led to the parking lot from the kitchen. "Yesterday morning the lock had been tampered with and the door had been ajar." She returned her gaze to Ryan. "Do you think anyone could have come in and messed with the chicken?"

Ryan went to the door, opened it, then examined it. He looked over his shoulder at Megan. "Do you have a security camera?"

Megan shook her head. "I don't think so."

"We don't." Margaret looked up from the vegetables she was chopping.

"Maybe we should get one," Tess said and Megan nodded in agreement.

"I want to check out a couple of things." Ryan returned to Megan's side and gave her a quick kiss. "I'll be back in a while."

She nodded. "All right."

Ryan headed out the back door and closed it behind him. He stepped back and surveyed it before looking at the back of the Chuck Wagon on one side and the new convenience store on the other.

He studied the convenience store. They usually had plenty of cameras around. Maybe they had one that had a view of the café. He walked closer to the store and looked along the side. There was a camera on one corner. Depending on the angle it showed, there was a possibility that it had a view of the back door of the café.

Ryan walked to the convenience store, the smell of gas strong from the pumps out front. An electronic tone greeted him as he pushed the glass doors open. He didn't recognize the male clerk at the cash register.

"Who's the on-duty manager?" Ryan asked the clerk whose

nametag read, *Stuckey*.

"I am." Stuckey leaned on the counter. "What can I do for you?"

"I'd like to take a look at the surveillance recordings from the camera on the northwest corner of the building," Ryan said. "From Thursday night to Friday morning."

Stuckey shook his head. "No can do."

"It's important." Ryan tried to hold back his impatience.

The man shrugged. "Isn't everything?"

Ryan rested one forearm on the countertop. "Who's the owner?"

"Max Johnson," Stuckey said. "He's on vacation in the Bahamas."

Damn, Ryan thought, but only said, "Thanks," and pushed away from the counter. He walked outside the store and strode toward his truck behind the café.

After he unlocked the door, climbed in, and started the vehicle, he headed to the Yavapai County Sheriff's Department.

The drive wasn't far from the café and his luck held—his cousin, Sheriff Mike McBride, was in the office.

Mike greeted him after the receptionist let him know that Ryan was in to see him. Mike motioned for Ryan to follow him into his office.

"How are you doing these days?" Mike said as he sat behind his desk.

Ryan took a seat on one of the chairs in front of the desk. "Damned good." He leaned forward and braced his forearms on his thighs. "But there's a problem."

Mike nodded. "Go on."

"I'm sure you've heard about the food poisoning last night at the Hummingbird Café," Ryan said.

"I imagine everyone in the county has heard that news by now," Mike said. "What about it?"

"I think the chicken was tampered with." Ryan took off his western hat and held it. "I believe it was intentionally sabotaged."

Mike raised his brows. "Why don't you start from the beginning?"

"I think the beginning goes back a ways." Ryan told Mike about the Dysons winning the lease out from under Meyer and his threat that they would regret it.

"Are you saying Roger Meyer is responsible?" Mike said. "He's one big sonofabitch, but that's a pretty strong accusation."

"There's more," Ryan said. He explained about the poker game and Meyer's comments about the restaurant and his desire to get the lease on it. "He as much as told me what he was going to do when he said that maybe some people would get sick."

Mike's expression remained calm but his eyes hardened. "Anything more than his comment?"

"One of his friends from the poker game was hired as the Dysons' new cook," Ryan said. "His first day was yesterday, the day of the grand reopening and he cooked all of the chicken dinners." Ryan paused. "He didn't show up for work today."

Mike's gaze remained fixed on Ryan. "Got anything else?"

"The restaurant was broken into yesterday morning," Ryan said. "The Dysons couldn't find anything missing or tampered with, so they didn't report it."

"They have a security camera?" Mike asked.

Ryan shook his head. "No, but the convenience store next

door does, and I think the parking lot behind the café might be in the radius the camera covers. I talked with the clerk but he wouldn't let me take a look at the recordings."

Mike leaned forward. "Well then, I think a visit to the convenience store is in order."

After Mike grabbed his western hat, he and Ryan headed out of the sheriff's office. Ryan followed the sheriff's SUV to the convenience store where they both parked. They went in together.

"Hi, Stuckey." Mike pushed up the brim of his cowboy hat. "How's the wife and kids?"

"They're doing fine." Stuckey grinned at the sheriff. "What can I do for you, Sheriff McBride?"

Mike explained about the recordings he wanted to view.

"The boss is on vacation," Stuckey said, "but I wager he'd let you take a look at them. I can't leave so I'll have Les take you to the back."

Mike thanked him and Stuckey paged Les who showed up moments later. Stuckey told Les to let the sheriff look over anything he wanted to.

Les escorted Mike and Ryan to the back, past crates of merchandise that hadn't been stocked yet. It smelled of floor cleaner from the mop bucket they passed that was off to one side.

In the back office, Les showed them the security cameras. Sure enough, the one on the northwest corner had a partial view of the café's parking lot. Les searched that camera's recordings for the approximate time they were looking for.

"Sometime after dark on Thursday night," Ryan said. "The restaurant wasn't reopened until Friday morning, but Margaret Dyson and her daughters were at the café to accept deliveries during the day on Thursday."

It took some time studying the tape. Around two AM Friday morning, a car drove into the parking lot behind the café. Both Mike and Ryan leaned forward.

"Looks like an old Chevy Impala," Mike said. "Probably a 2001 or 2002."

They watched as a man climbed out of the car. His face was shadowed and they couldn't get a good look. The man went around the back of the car, opened the trunk, and took out a box before slamming the trunk lid shut.

The man's face was still shadowed until he walked into the light from the pole behind the café.

"That's him." Ryan leaned back as his suspicion was confirmed. "It's Julian Taylor."

Ryan and Mike watched as Taylor set down the box then messed with the lock at the back door. Moments later, he opened the door, picked up the box, and headed into the café. About ten minutes later, Taylor came out of the restaurant holding a box, then went back to the Impala where he put the box in the back then climbed into the driver's seat.

"I've seen enough." Mike stopped the tape. "I have enough to arrest this Julian Taylor."

"Mind of I tag along?" Ryan asked his cousin. "I can identify him."

"After I get a warrant, you can be there when we make the arrest," Mike said.

Mike thanked Les and Stuckey and went outside with Ryan. They headed to his office and Mike arranged for a warrant. While they waited, he got what he needed to track down Taylor.

When Mike had the information and the warrant, he arranged for backup to meet him at Taylor's apartment.

"If the man's home it'll save us some time chasing him down," Mike said to Ryan before they headed on out.

When they reached the apartment complex, Mike and Ryan waited for the deputy to arrive as backup. When Deputy Choate arrived, the three of them went to Taylor's apartment door. Ryan stayed back as Mike knocked.

After a few knocks, Taylor came to the door wearing a white wife-beater T-shirt. He looked rumpled and bleary eyed, like he was stinking drunk. The moment he got a look at the badge on Mike's belt and saw the deputy behind him, his entire demeanor changed. He straightened, his knuckles whitening as he gripped the doorframe with one hand, his other hand holding the door.

"I'm Sheriff McBride," Mike said. "Are you Julian Taylor?"

The man licked his lips. "Yes."

Mike gave the deputy a signal before he said, "Julian Taylor, we have a warrant for your arrest."

Taylor looked like he was about to wet his pants. "For what?"

"For breaking and entering," Mike said as the deputy grabbed Taylor by his arm, jerked him out of the doorway, and cuffed him.

"What are you talking about?" Taylor said, his voice shaking.

The deputy started reading Taylor his Miranda rights.

Mike nodded to the deputy. "Get him out of here."

Ryan and Mike stood on the opposite side of the one-way mirror as they studied Taylor who sat at a bare wooden table in the interrogation room. His head was hanging as he stared at his lap, his wrists cuffed behind him.

"Let's see what he has to say." Mike clapped Ryan on the shoulder then left Ryan standing in the viewing room.

Ryan watched as Mike walked into the interrogation room.

Mike moved in front of the table "I understand you've waived your right for an attorney."

"I don't have anything to hide," Taylor said but looked nervous. "I'm innocent."

"Why did you break into the Hummingbird Café, Julian?" Mike asked.

"I didn't break into the café," Taylor said, and his throat worked as he swallowed.

"We know you broke in," Mike said. "We want to know why."

Taylor's knee bounced showing his nervousness. "I told you I didn't break in."

"We have a tape from a security camera showing you breaking in." Mike sat in the chair on the opposite side of the table from Taylor.

The man went still as his face went white. "I—I left my cell phone there and I went back to get it."

"Dumb story. This will go a lot better for you if you tell the truth," Mike said. "What was in that box you carried in?"

Taylor looked like words were stuck in his throat.

"It was chicken," Mike stated. "Planting tainted chicken is a felony so you're doing some serious jail time, Taylor. You got a lot of people sick."

"No." Taylor shook his head. "I'd never—"

"Tell you what," Mike said. "We might be able to strike a deal. You tell me everything, including who you were working for, and you'll get less jail time. We know you didn't do this on your own."

Taylor looked even more panicked. "I—I can't go to jail."

"That's exactly where you're going if you don't come clean, Julian," Mike said. "Now tell me all of it, from the beginning."

"You said you could give me a deal?" Knee still bouncing, Taylor licked his lips. "What kind of deal can you give me?"

"We'll take your cooperation into consideration, depending on what you tell us," Mike said.

"Okay, I'll tell you everything." Taylor sucked in his breath then let his words out in a rush. "I didn't know all those people were going to get sick."

"Go on," Mike said.

A sheen of sweat was on Taylor's forehead as he spoke. "Roger Meyer paid me to replace the chicken in the Hummingbird Café with the chicken in the box."

Mike's expression didn't change. "Do you have any proof?"

Taylor looked like he was thinking about it for a moment and then he said, "Roger gave me instructions. I still have all of the text messages."

Ryan gave a grim smile as he listened to Taylor spill even more information about Meyer.

"He had his reporter cousin write bad reviews, too," Taylor said in a rush. "He planned out everything."

When he finished, Mike turned off the tape recorder and came out of the interrogation room.

"He sure folded fast," Ryan said as soon as Mike closed the door behind him.

Mike gave a nod. "He's not a professional and doesn't have a record. He was scared shitless. Looks like you were right about Meyer."

Ryan felt some satisfaction. The bastard was going down.

CHAPTER 26

Roger Meyer came into the restaurant and walked straight past Megan who had been straightening the menus at the hostess stand.

Anger surged through her. "Where are you going?"

The man ignored her and headed into the kitchen. She followed, trying to keep up with him, but his legs were long and he strode ahead of her.

When she reached the kitchen, Meyer was face to face with her mother. Margaret was holding a spatula up and looked like she was going to hit him with it.

"Get out of my kitchen," Margaret demanded, her eyes red-rimmed from stress and exhaustion.

"You poisoned a hell of a lot of people," Meyer said with a

smirk. "Your business will never recover from it. The smart thing to do is let me take over your lease before you lose everything."

Margaret's wore a furious expression. "Go to hell."

"I'll get it sooner or later." Meyer laughed. "Might as well do it before you're in so much debt you won't be able to crawl out of it."

Margaret straightened and raised her chin. "Get out of my kitchen."

"It won't be yours much longer." Meyer smiled.

Megan stepped closer and opened her mouth to echo her mother and kick Meyer out, but a man walked past her, catching her off guard. She didn't get a good look at the man who wore a Stetson, a leather jacket, and Wrangler jeans.

The man said, "Hello, Roger."

Meyer turned, his face registering some surprise before he put on a fake pleasant expression. "Good afternoon, Sheriff McBride."

Megan blinked. She sensed more men behind her and stepped out of the way as a deputy passed her. Ryan was standing in the kitchen doorway, watching.

Confused, Megan gave the sheriff and deputy more space.

"Roger, I have a warrant for your arrest," Sheriff McBride said then gave a nod to the deputy who approached Meyer.

"What the hell?" Meyer jerked away from the deputy.

"Do we need to add resisting arrest to the other charges?" the sheriff asked.

Meyer's jaw tightened as he let the deputy cuff him. "What charges?"

The sheriff started listing charges and Megan's eyes widened. Meyer was being arrested for tainted chicken being planted in the restaurant. He had been the one to poison all of those people.

When the sheriff finished, the deputy read Meyer his Miranda rights. The man clenched his teeth, his face red with anger.

A news cameraman entered and started recording Meyer's arrest.

"I wish Paul was here to see this," Margaret said. "You all but killed him."

Meyer gave Margaret a furious glare but said nothing as the deputy pushed past the cameraman and escorted him out of the kitchen. Meyer saw Ryan and his angry expression intensified.

The cameraman followed Meyer through the restaurant as the deputy took him out to the waiting cruiser.

Margaret smiled. "Thank you, Sheriff."

Sheriff McBride glanced at Ryan. "Thank Ryan here. He figured it all out and put it together."

Margaret walked up to Ryan and looked at him a moment before she hugged him. When she stepped back, she smiled at him and wiped a tear from her eyes. "We really had the wrong impression of you. I'm sorry." She brushed away another tear. "Thank you."

When the sheriff left, Megan went into Ryan's arms, so much relief pouring through her that she could barely stand it. She lifted her face to his and he kissed her until her head spun with it.

* * * * *

Megan unfolded the newspaper on the hostess stand and found yet another article covering everything that had transpired over the past year, culminating with the poisoning of multiple individuals.

Roger Meyer's vendetta against the Hummingbird Café made

front-page news in Prescott. News stations and newspapers in Phoenix picked up the story about how Meyer had paid someone to plant tainted chicken in the café, which had caused more than twenty people to come down with food poisoning.

More information came out about the extent of Meyer's mission to take down the café. He'd paid a reporter to give the café bad reviews in the Prescott Review and had written multiple bad reviews from non-existent patrons.

All of which had nearly devastated the small family restaurant.

Meyer was going to prison. His own restaurant, Chuck Wagon, had been shut down.

Tess and Margaret walked into the dining room as Megan opened the newspaper she was holding to the Lifestyle section.

Megan's jaw dropped. She looked up at her mother and sister. "There's a feature article written about the history of our family's café in Albuquerque and how successful it was before the business was moved to Prescott."

"Really?" Tess went up to Megan and leaned over her shoulder. "It talks about how the restaurant received four and five star reviews from customers and media outlets and how the food and service were award winning."

"That's fantastic." Margaret beamed as she joined Megan and Tess.

Megan folded up the newspaper and tucked it away in the hostess station. "Hopefully that will all be good for our second grand re-reopening."

"I'm sure it will," Tess said with a broad smile.

Today was a special day. Not only was it the grand re-reopening, but the restaurant was holding a fundraiser to help Mary Jane Dow pay her medical bills. Her son, Bill, was so grateful he'd been working as often as he could to help the café prepare for the fundraiser whenever Ryan could spare him. Ryan had been great about letting Bill have extra time off.

Margaret had hired two waitresses for the evening but Megan was there today because an unusually large crowd was hoped for. The new cook came with a sterling recommendation from a Phoenix restaurant and had extensive credentials that they'd verified. After Julian Taylor, they weren't taking any chances.

Bells jangled and in walked Mr. Cowell, owner of the buildings that Meyer and the Dysons leased.

"Good morning," Margaret said to the balding man with a broad smile.

"How are you doing, Mrs. Dyson?" the man asked. "And you as well, ladies?" he nodded at Tess and Megan.

"Great," Megan and Tess each said at the same time then smiled at each other.

"Just fine," Margaret said. "What can I do for you?"

"I have a proposition for you," Mr. Cowell said. "I'd like to lease to you the building that the Chuck Wagon occupied. I can offer you a special rate."

Margaret looked intrigued. "What would that be?"

He told her and added, "I'd be willing to give you free rent at the front end to help get your business turned around. I realize you've suffered a setback with all that happened, but I have a good feeling that your restaurant will recover and prosper."

"Thank you," Margaret said. "I'll give it some serious consideration and get back with you."

The man smiled. "I'll see you tonight at your grand reopening."

"Grand re-reopening," Tess said with a laugh.

Both Tess and Margaret headed back to the kitchen after Mr. Cowell left.

As they returned to their duties, Megan thought about the invitation that had just arrived this morning. She fished it out of her purse, which she'd temporarily put behind the hostess station. She looked at the fancy script on the heavy paper. Her ex-sister-in-law, Christine, and her fiancé, Todd, were getting married in a month.

She smiled to herself. The pain that used to accompany thoughts of Bart had all but vanished. She would love to see her ex-in-laws and she shouldn't let a little thing like her ex-husband ruin her friendship with Grace, Montgomery, and Christine.

Bells jangled at the door and Megan looked up to see Ryan coming through the door. Every time she saw him, she felt warmth flow through her and her heart filled in a way that gave her a feeling of completeness that she'd never felt before.

He gave her the sexy smile, which sent familiar butterflies through her belly. She went to him and he took her into his arms and gave her a kiss that set her senses on fire.

When he stepped back she handed him the invitation. "My ex-sister-in-law is getting married." He took the folded paper from her. "Would you like to go with me?" she asked.

He smiled and looked at the invitation. "Whatever the date is, I'll make it work."

She wrapped her arms around his neck. "Thank you."

He put his hands on her waist and his forehead against hers. "I'd go anywhere for you."

* * * * *

The night had been successful beyond their expectations. There was even a thirty-minute wait and no one seemed to be bothered by the length of time it would take to be seated.

Thirty percent of the night's profits were going to the fund for Mary Jane Dow and there was also a large acrylic box that filled with donations throughout the evening. Meg watched, nearly overwhelmed by the outpouring from the community, as the level of cash rose and rose.

It was so busy that even Ryan had good naturedly put on an apron and helped in the kitchen.

When the last patron had left for the evening, Megan, Tess, Margaret, and Ryan sat at a table.

"What a night," Margaret said.

"It was incredible," Tess said. "It blew away our last re-opening and that one was a huge success."

"Ryan," Margaret said, and he turned his attention to her. "I've been thinking about the proposal you and your uncle made about the house." She took a deep breath. "I want to sell the house and get a smaller place. Now that Paul's gone, I don't need such a big house. So do whatever you need to and I'm sure everything will work out fine."

Megan reached out and put her hand over her mother's and smiled. "Yes, everything will be more than fine."

CHAPTER 27

Ryan linked his fingers through Megan's as they stood in the last pew in the church while Todd and Christine were pronounced husband and wife by the preacher. It was a beautiful wedding and her ex-sister-in-law was a gorgeous bride in a white beaded gown with a sheer veil over her long dark curls.

As Christine and Todd came down the aisle, Ryan put his arm around Megan's shoulders and held her close to him. She tilted her head to look up at him and he kissed her smile.

When he drew away, she slipped her arm around his waist as the newly married couple passed them and stepped through the huge double doors to their new life just waiting for them.

Megan caught sight of Bart on the other side of the aisle and noted that he was watching her and wearing a frown. When her eyes met his, she realized she had no feelings of any kind. No feelings of pain or dislike. She felt…nothing. Bart was a part of a distant life, a past that had healed. She smiled and turned away, but she could still feel his gaze on her.

The reception was being held in a hall just off the church and she walked hand in hand with Ryan to the huge hall decorated in vivid blues, the wedding colors, and white. Paper bells and streamers hung from the ceiling and tables were decorated with white and blue bouquets.

A live band was in one corner and the music started just as Ryan and Megan walked into the hall. Ryan took her into his arms and swept her onto the dance floor. Megan wore a lovely royal purple dress that swirled around her ankles as they danced.

She laughed and looked up at him. "You know more than country dancing. I had no idea."

He gave her a grin. "I'm full of surprises, honey."

She smiled back at him. "Yes, you are."

They spent the evening dancing and talking with Megan's ex-in-laws. They hugged Megan and seemed genuinely pleased to see her again and to meet Ryan.

As they danced around the hall, she caught glimpses of Bart watching her. She ignored him and focused on Ryan and the happiness that filled her heart.

After another dance, Megan excused herself to go to the ladies' room. She took a tube of lipstick out of her purse and looked at her reflection in the mirror as she freshened up her makeup. The door to the room squeaked and from her side vision she saw Bart's girlfriend, Barb, walk in.

Megan put her lipstick back into her purse. When she looked

up, Barb was standing beside her, startling Megan.

Barb was a blonde bombshell with a beautiful figure and face. There was a time when Megan would have been envious of the woman, but those days were long gone. She wouldn't trade her life for anything now. Besides, Barb had Bart. Megan figured she would have felt sorry for Barb if the woman hadn't had an affair with her husband. They deserved each other.

But then again, Barb actually had done Megan a big favor.

"Megan, right?" Barb cocked her head.

"Yes," Megan said. "And you're Barb."

The woman gave a nod. "Tell me what happened between you two."

"Really?" Megan blinked at her in surprise. "You, of course."

Barb frowned. "What other things were there that made your marriage bad? Because it wasn't good, was it." She said the last as a statement, not a question.

Megan paused. "I really don't want to talk about it. That's ancient history."

"I want to know." Barb clenched her hand on the countertop. "Did he call you names or verbally abuse you in other ways?"

Megan adjusted her purse on her shoulder. "Listen, Barb, that's ancient history for me."

"Well, it's not for me." Barb's eyes looked red—either from anger or tears, Megan wasn't sure.

"Like I said," Megan repeated, "ancient history."

Barb gave a nod. "I thought so. That's the kind of bastard he is."

"I concluded a while ago that Bart isn't going to change," Megan said. "Bart is Bart. I'm sorry to tell you that, but I suspect you know it already."

Barb spun and marched out of the bathroom, anger on her features.

Megan shook her head. "That was weird," she said under her breath.

As she walked back into the hall she saw Barb snatch her purse and her shawl from the chair beside the one Bart was occupying.

His chair nearly toppled as he got to his feet in a rush. Barb kept her voice down but it was clear she was furious with Bart. She turned and stormed out of the hall with Bart hurrying after her.

Megan mentally shrugged and went back to Ryan who handed her a cup of punch.

Moments later, Bart returned and strode to where Megan stood with Ryan. Bart ignored Ryan. To Megan he said, "What did you say to Barb?"

Megan studied him. "I said nothing to her. If you're having problems, it's your doing, Bart, not mine. Now please excuse us."

Bart's face was red. He stepped closer to Megan and opened his mouth, probably to spout some kind of insult, but Ryan stepped between them.

"Excuse us," Ryan echoed. He put his arm around Megan's shoulders and escorted her onto the dance floor. It was a slow dance and he held her close.

"Thank you." Megan let out a breath of relief. "That could have gone poorly."

"Not while I'm around." He studied her eyes. "Was that your ex?"

She nodded. "I've never told you anything about him other than the fact that I was married. Bart was a part of my past I wanted to forget. Now I don't care enough for it to matter."

Ryan gently stroked the side of her face. "If he ever bothers you again, you let me know, okay?"

She smiled and nodded. "All right."

The night ended beautifully and after the reception they returned to the exquisite hotel they were staying in.

When they reached their room, Megan slipped out of her dressy coat and dropped it over a chair. She went to the floor to ceiling windows, pulled aside the curtains, and opened the sliding door to go out onto the balcony.

Ryan came up behind her and put his hands at her waist and rested his chin on her shoulder and looked at the city lights spread out below them.

"It's beautiful." Megan breathed in the crisp night air and shivered. Snow was in the forecast for Albuquerque.

"Come in before you freeze," he murmured and she felt his warm breath as he kissed her neck.

She let him take her hand and draw her back into the room. Cold air swirled into the warm room as he closed the door behind them. She went straight into his arms and felt the heat of his body that chased any chill away.

He nuzzled her neck then drew away. She tilted her head back and he brought his mouth to hers. It was both a sweet and a hungry kiss.

When he raised his head, he brushed her hair away from her face. "I'm going to say something I've been waiting to say for the longest time."

Her breathing hitched as she looked up at him, her lips parted and wet from his kiss.

"I don't know why I took so long to tell you this. God knows I've known this forever." He cupped the side of her face and ran his thumb along her lower lip. "I love you, Megan. I love you more than I could ever have believed."

Her heart beat faster as warmth traveled through her. She was so overwhelmed with emotion she almost couldn't speak.

She flung her arms around his neck. "I love you, Ryan. I love you, love you, love you."

He grinned, picked her up by her waist and swung her around. She squealed with surprise and laughter. She was unsteady on her feet when he set her down, but he didn't let her go. He wrapped her tight in his arms and rocked her from side to side, causing her to laugh again.

"You do know I'm never letting you go, don't you?" he said.

"Don't worry," she said as she smiled up at him. "I won't let you."

He pushed the strap of her dress aside and kissed her shoulder as he moved one hand to her zipper. She shivered as he slid it down to her waist. He stepped back just enough to help her slide the straps down her arms and fall to her feet in a shimmering purple mass.

When he saw her in her black corset, garters, stockings, and heels, he sucked in his breath. "Damn, that's sexy," he said and reached around to grab her ass cheeks through her silky black panties and pulled her up hard against him.

"I'm glad you like," she said as she felt his rigid cock against her belly.

His blue eyes had darkened with passion. "I love."

She ran her hands along his shoulders. "Take off your clothes."

He shrugged out of the western suit jacket he'd worn for the wedding and tossed it onto a chair. He toed off his boots, stripped out of his dress shirt and belt, then pushed down his pants and boxer briefs.

When he was naked, he scooped up Megan and laid her on the bed. "I want you to wear all of this while I take you." He ran one hand down her corset to her hip, over her garter and down her silky stockings and back up to the top of her corset again.

He pulled down the top of the corset and freed her breasts. She gasped and slid her fingers into his hair as he sucked on each of her nipples. He reached between them, pulled her panties aside, and placed his cock against her core.

With his eyes holding hers, he pushed inside of her. She moaned as he entered her. He moved in and out, slow and even.

He thrust harder as he looked into her eyes, her breasts bouncing with the movement. Their lovemaking grew even more intense as her hips rose up to meet his and she met his every stroke.

Megan's orgasm built and built until she was almost to the peak. He thrust hard and deep.

"I love you, Megan," he said and she fell over the cliff, her body shuddering with the impact of her orgasm. Her body throbbed and vibrated as his strokes continued.

"I love you, Ryan." She saw his eyes darken even more. "I love you."

His shout echoed through the room as he came hard, his expression fierce as he pressed his groin to hers.

He braced his hands to either side of her as he stayed inside of her until his breathing calmed and the beating of her heart finally slowed.

And then he moved onto his side and took her into his arms and held her.

CHAPTER 28

"I can't." Megan shook her head and balked as Ryan tugged her toward the Ferris wheel that rose up in the night, lit with bright lights that blinked in invitation. "I've told you, those things scare me to death."

"It's perfectly safe and I won't rock it." Ryan gave her a quick kiss. "Promise."

Megan's heart pounded at the thought of riding the dreaded thing. She looked up into his denim blue eyes and saw love there and she couldn't refuse him.

"For you." She gave him a shaky smile.

"Come on then." He grinned and squeezed her hand as they walked down the crowded midway, through the brilliantly lit carnival, and toward the monstrosity that they called a Ferris wheel.

It was their one-year anniversary since having met at this very place, the carnival at the county fair. And now she was going to brave her biggest fear.

And conquer it. Yes, she would.

She hoped.

When they reached the Ferris wheel, she felt jittery as they stood in line. Ryan dug tickets out of his pocket. She squeezed his hand tighter when it was their turn to get into one of the seats that had stopped at the bottom, ready for them to climb in. Ryan let her in first and he slid in next to her and put his arm around her shoulders.

Something about his touch gave her a sense of security that calmed her fears. She leaned on his shoulder and he kissed the top of her head.

The wheel jerked as it started to move to let the next passengers on. As they rose she took deep breaths and let them out. She found her breathing was calmer and her heart didn't pound as hard while she was within the security of Ryan's arm.

They reached the very top of the Ferris wheel and Megan looked out over the sea of people below, absorbing the flashing lights, color and carnival sounds—music and the cries of carnies calling to each passerby.

She looked beyond the carnival. The view extended for miles, city lights glittering in the darkness.

"I have something for you," he murmured in her ear.

She tilted her head to look up at him. "And what would that be?"

He slid his hand into his jeans pocket and pulled out a square velvet box.

Her heart started pounding again, for an entirely different reason.

He opened the box and there, set against black velvet, was a diamond solitaire.

The Ferris wheel started to slowly turn, but she barely noticed it as she raised her gaze from the diamond to meet his eyes.

"I've wanted to wait for the right time to ask you and I think where we met is the perfect place. " He smiled as lights flashed around them. "I love you with everything I am, Megan. Will you marry me?"

"I love you, Ryan." She wrapped her arms around his neck, mindless of the swaying of the seat that her movements caused. "Of course I'll marry you, a thousand times over."

He kissed her long and hard, then drew away. He took her hand and slid the ring on her finger and surprisingly, it fit perfectly. "Tess gave me your ring size," he said.

"Tess knew?" Megan laughed as she looked at the diamond on her finger. "No wonder she looked like she was about to burst with something when I left. She wouldn't tell me what was going on. Now I know."

Her ring sparkled in the flashing lights as she leaned on his shoulder.

"How about kids?" he asked and she brought her attention to his. "We can start as soon as we're married. And I want to be married to you as soon as possible."

Children. Just like she'd always wanted.

Her smile broadened. "We can practice just as soon as we get home."

* * * * *

Before they headed home, Megan and Ryan stopped at her mother's restaurant and bar. With the success of the Hummingbird Café, they'd expanded into the part of the building formerly occupied by Roger Meyer's Chuck Wagon.

They passed Nectars, the bar section of the restaurant which was now just called the Hummingbird. Laughter and music spilled out onto the sidewalk from the bar.

Megan looked up at Ryan. "It's amazing how incredible the place is doing," she said.

"Considering the award-winning cuisine and nightlife, it's not surprising at all," he said as they reached the entrance of the Hummingbird. "And the peach pies." He grinned down at her. "Your mom's peach pies are the best ever."

She nodded. "The Hummingbird and Nectars deserve the success."

Ryan opened the door and held it open as Megan walked through. She greeted the hostess as they passed by and headed for the kitchen. Servers took care of their full tables and the restaurant was filled with the clinking of silverware and conversation.

When they reached the kitchen, Megan spotted her mother moving through the place, keeping an eye on everything. Margaret was as hands-on as an owner could get, and still dove in wherever needed.

"Mom." Megan caught Margaret's attention.

Margaret smiled and dried her hands on a dishtowel as she walked across the kitchen to where Megan was standing, Ryan at her side.

"How are you doing, Margaret?" Ryan asked when she

reached them.

"A little worn out, but otherwise just fine." She tucked the dishtowel into a pocket of her apron. "What are you two doing tonight?"

Megan raised her hand and showed her mother the sparkling diamond on her finger.

Delight lit up Margaret's face. "That's wonderful!" She hugged Megan then held her by her shoulders and said, "You couldn't have found a better man."

Megan looked up at Ryan. "I know."

"I couldn't have found a better woman." Ryan hugged Margaret. "She means everything to me."

Margaret and Ryan parted, her mother still smiling as she looked from Ryan to Megan. "I wish your father was here to see you both. I think once he got to know you, he would have welcomed you into the family just as much as I do."

"I would have liked getting to know him," Ryan said and rested his arm around Megan's shoulders.

"Are you going anywhere to celebrate?" Margaret asked, her hands clasped in front of her.

"We thought we'd celebrate right here." Megan gave a nod to the dining room before turning back to her mother. "We couldn't think of a better place to be."

"Wonderful." Margaret looked away from them. "Tess," she called out.

Tess came out of the back office and grinned as she came toward them. "I see you've got a little sparkle there."

"Good job keeping a secret." Megan raised her hand so that Tess could get a good look at the ring.

"It's gorgeous." Tess hugged Megan then Ryan.

"They're celebrating here," Margaret said with pride.

Tess gave a broad smile. "Then you shall have the best seat in the house and the best champagne we have."

Even though Megan knew every seat in the place, she and Ryan followed Tess to a corner table and Tess gestured to it. "Order anything you like and the chef will make it for you."

Megan laughed as Ryan seated her. "You might regret that offer."

"Never," Tess said before she smiled and left.

When Ryan had taken his seat beside her, he grasped her hand in his and looked at the ring before meeting her gaze. "I love seeing my ring on you. It can't begin to say how much I love you."

She squeezed his hand and smiled. She wanted to get up and dance and dance. She felt like a million stars were inside her, glittering through her whole being. She wouldn't be surprised if she glowed with it.

She leaned forward and kissed him, letting him feel her glow in the magic that seemed to surround them.

When they drew back but a breath, she smiled against his lips. "I love you," she whispered and kissed him again.

ALSO BY CHEYENNE MCCRAY

"Riding Tall" Series

Branded For You

"Rough and Ready" Series

Silk and Spurs
Lace and Lassos
Champagne and Chaps
Satin and Saddles
Roses and Rodeo
Lingerie and Lariats
Lipstick and Leather

"Altered States" Series

Dark Seduction

"Dark Enforcers" Series

Night's Captive

Lexi Steele Novels

The First Sin
The Second Betrayal
The Temptation

From St. Martin's Press:

"Night Tracker" Series

Demons Not Included
No Werewolves Allowed
Vampires Not Invited
Zombies Sold Separately
Vampires Dead Ahead

"Magic" Series

Forbidden Magic
Seduced by Magic
Wicked Magic
Shadow Magic
Dark Magic

Single Title

Moving Target
Chosen Prey

Anthologies

No Rest for the Witches
Real Men Last All Night
Legally Hot
Chicks Kick Butt
Hotter than Hell
Mammoth Book of Paranormal Romances
Mammoth Book of Special Ops Romances

Cheyenne writing as
Jaymie Holland

Excerpt... Lingerie and Lariats

Cheyenne McCray

When they'd finished dinner and washed up the dishes, she walked with him to the living room. They paused and stood in the center of the room as he studied her and she met his eyes. Her belly flip-flopped at his intense gaze. He looked her as if she was a treasure he wanted to protect.

But at the same time he looked at her like a man who wanted a woman. A look of passion and need was in his gaze that couldn't be disguised.

He reached up and ran strands of her long hair through his fingers. "I want to kiss you, Renee."

She bit the inside of her lip as her own need expanded inside her. She slid her hands up his chest to his shoulders and offered him a smile. "I want you to."

His warm breath feathered across her lips as he lowered his mouth to hers. The intensity of the moment was filled with a kind of fire that made her burn inside.

Her eyelids fluttered closed as he brought his mouth to hers, and it was like magic sparked between them when their lips met. She felt as if her mind was spinning and stars glittered behind her eyes. She fell into the kiss, her head whirling, her heart pounding.

His taste made her want more of him and she made sounds of need and pleasure. He deepened the kiss and she gave a soft moan.

She reveled in his embrace, the feel of his hard chest against her breasts and the warmth and comfort of his arms around her. She strained to somehow get closer to him, to become a part of him.

A deep, rumbling groan rose up in him and he kissed her hard before drawing away. He still held her in his embrace and she loved the feeling of security she experienced in his arms.

She opened her eyes and stared up at him, her lips moist from his kiss, her breathing a little fast.

He gently brushed hair from her cheek as he looked down at her, and his expression turned serious. "I've wanted to kiss you from the moment I first saw you at the Cameron's place, but I shouldn't have done that. I don't want to take advantage of you in a vulnerable state."

For a long moment she looked up at him, studying the sea green of his eyes. "When I was a young girl, living with the Camerons, I had the biggest crush on you."

The corner of his mouth quirked into a smile. "Is that so?" he said in a lazy drawl.

She returned his smile. "When you saved my life, you became my hero as well as my crush."

"I thought you were pretty cute." He slid his fingers into her hair and cupped the back of her head. "And you've grown up to be one hell of a beautiful woman."

She placed her hands on his chest, reached up on her toes, and kissed him. His lips were firm and he returned her kiss, his kiss as hungry as hers. Searching, longing, and filled with desire. She gripped his shirt in her hands as she pressed her body tight to his. She didn't think she could get enough of him.

Judging by the hard ridge she felt against her belly, she knew he was as affected as she was by the moment.

He drew away again and she felt his rapid heartbeat against her palm and his chest rose and fell with the increased pace of his breathing.

"It was a mistake to kiss you because it only makes me want more. A lot more." He slid his fingers through her long, glossy hair. "I want so much more of you than that. But it's too soon."

She closed her eyes, letting her breathing slow. When she opened them again she found him watching her. Her voice seemed a little shaky. "You're right, it's too soon. All of this with Jerry has been so emotional. I'm feeling everything right now… Hate and anger for him, and strong feelings for you. But I shouldn't take things so fast no matter how right it feels with you." She brushed her fingers along his shirt collar. "And Dan, it feels so right."

"It feels unbelievably right." He lowered his head and gave her a firm, hard kiss then stepped back. Her palms slid down his chest and then he took her hands in his. "How about watching a movie and getting our minds off of certain things?"

"That sounds like a good idea." Not that she thought she could get her mind off of wanting to experience more with Dan. She gestured to the front door. "Why don't we watch the storm first?"

He took her small hand in his big one and they went outside onto the covered porch and closed the front door behind them. Patches of warm yellow light spilled from the house onto the porch.

The sky was dark, the occasional crack of lighting illuminating the trees and outbuildings for seconds before everything went dark again. The air smelled fresh and clean as wind pressed her clothing against her body and her hair rose up off her shoulders. A gust of wind sent a mist of wetness onto the porch and she smiled at the feel of warm summer rain on her skin.

As they watched the storm, he squeezed her hand and looked down at her. She met his gaze and smiled. They stood on the porch a while longer and she watched bolts of lightning slicing the sky as thunder rolled across the valley.

EXCERPT... ROSES AND RODEO

Cheyenne McCray

"No thank you." Danica turned down yet another offer from a cowboy to buy her a drink.

After she declined, she dismissed the cowboy with a genuine smile. She moved away to search the room with her gaze for Kelsey. She held onto her beer bottle as she moved through the crowd.

The bar was packed with men and women in western attire and a country-western band had been playing familiar tunes all night. She liked that the slot machines were outside the bar and the constant ringing and cha-ching of machines wasn't competing with the good music.

She'd caught herself lightly tapping her boot since she'd come into the bar, but she hadn't been in the mood to dance. Usually she did, but tonight she had a headache that alcohol hadn't been able to kick. Thank goodness smoking had been banned from bars and restaurants in Las Vegas or her headache would have magnified.

Her gaze slid past Creed who had three women around him. Kelsey had called the women buckle bunnies, female groupies. From what she'd seen, the groupies tended to wear tight jeans and boots with skimpy tops and bright, flashy accessories like a belt with a big buckle that had lots of dazzle.

She moved her gaze away from the cowboy and groupies then spotted her petite friend who was leaning against Darryl, her hand on his chest, looking into the tall cowboy's eyes. It was a sweet, romantic picture the way he was looking at her. Danica hoped Kelsey wouldn't get her heart broken. She'd been through far too much and she deserved a good guy. Danica had met him earlier in the night when Kelsey had introduced them. He seemed okay, but she'd reserve judgment for later.

Her cell phone had vibrated in her pocket three separate times. She was sure they were messages from Barry, so she didn't bother to look.

From the corner of her eye, she found herself looking at Creed. This time a woman who looked upset was talking with him and the buckle bunnies were gone. He reached up and brushed something from beneath her eye with his thumb. He said something to her and she nodded, then turned and walked in Danica's direction. The woman bumped into Danica, nearly making her drop her beer bottle.

Danica took a step back and shook her head. She looked at Darryl and Kelsey again. They really did look like a cute couple. She glanced away from the pair to check her watch. It was still early but she really wasn't in the mood to party. Maybe she'd tell Kelsey about her headache and that she was going to head up to their suite in the casino resort hotel that was on the strip. She wouldn't mind a bath in the amazing jetted tub.

"Heading off so early?" The deep drawl caught her attention. She immediately loved the male voice and turned to find herself facing Creed McBride.

She raised her brows. "Who says I'm leaving?"

He gave a slow, sexy grin. "Honey, you've been trying to head out that door all night."

Her face warmed. "You've been watching me?"

"Ever since you walked into the room." He searched her gaze. "Just waiting for a chance to catch your attention. I don't think there's a cowboy in this place who hasn't offered to buy you a drink."

She studied his eyes. He had dark hair and nice eyes that were a gorgeous shade of green. "Who's to say I'm not going to send you packing?"

His gaze held hers. "I'm hoping my luck will hold out. I think this is the longest conversation you've had with any cowboy you've met tonight."

Amusement sparked in his eyes as he spoke. He had that same ease and confidence in his manner in person as she'd seen before he'd ridden that bull and even after his ride.

He was about as tall as her four brothers, around six-two, but a little younger—she'd guess about thirty-three. His white shirt and Wrangler jeans fit him oh-so-well, and his white western hat was tilted up enough that she could study his eyes. He was definitely hot in an alpha male, bad boy kinda way.

"I'm Creed McBride." He held out his hand.

"My name is Danica and you're right, I'm heading up to my room." She smiled as she took his hand. "Nice meeting you," she added but couldn't get herself to turn away. In fact she had a hard time getting herself to release his hand. His grip was firm and warm, his hand callused from hard work.

It was probably only seconds but it seemed as though it carried on longer before she finally drew back her hand.

"Pretty name." He looked like he wanted to touch her again to keep her from leaving but held himself back. She didn't know why she thought he did, but she could almost feel the brush of his fingers against her cheek even though he hadn't reached for her at all. He studied her and she felt warmth go through her at the intensity in her look. "I bet you're told all of the time what gorgeous blue eyes you have. Such a brilliant blue," he said.

"Is that a pick-up line?" She raised an eyebrow.

"You know it's not." He smiled. "It's an observation."

It was true that she got that all of the time. She and her four brothers had the same eye color and her aunt called them "Cameron blue".

"Are you sure you wouldn't like to two-step with me?" Creed gave a nod to the dance floor. "I haven't had a chance to dance all night."

She wanted to ask him why not when gorgeous women had surrounded him all night, or the other woman he'd been talking with, but she didn't want him to know that he'd captured her attention tonight, more than once. Fortunately, she didn't think he'd caught her at it.

Darryl came up to Creed's side and he put his arm around Creed's neck. "Do you know who you're talkin' to?" Darryl raised his beer bottle with his opposite hand. "You should be damned impressed. This is Creed McBride, two-time world bull riding champion."

Creed looked uncomfortable and Danica's lips twisted with amusement as she teased him. "I'm impressed by a lot of things, but riding an animal out to kill you isn't one of them. I'm more impressed by the person."

"Felt the heat on that one." A slight grin curved the corner of Creed's mouth, obviously knowing she was teasing, and he disengaged from Darryl. "Why don't you go find that cute little blonde you've been with all night?" he said to Darryl.

Darryl turned his gaze on Danica and slowly looked her up and down. Disgust flowed through her at the blatant way he was undressing her with his gaze. "What about this sexy thing?" He grinned. "Danica, right?"

"Yes." She folded her arms across her chest. "Best friend to Kelsey Richards. Where is she, by the way?"

Darryl jerked his thumb over his shoulder. "She's waiting for me by the bar."

Danica put her hands on her hips. "I think I might need to go have a talk with her."

"Just havin' a little fun." Darryl straightened. "I best be getting back to Kelsey."

Danica frowned, wondering if she *should* go have a talk with her friend. But then Danica wondered if maybe she was reading too much into the way he'd been looking at her.

Darryl touched the brim of his hat. "Ma'am," he said politely, his demeanor completely changed. Darryl slapped Creed on the shoulder then turned and headed toward the bar where Danica caught a glimpse of Kelsey.

"Come on." Creed indicated that dance floor with a nod. "Give this cowboy a dance."

The only indecision that warred within her was the thought of getting to know him better, maybe even liking him, when she'd already decided that she wouldn't want to date a bull rider. Not that dancing with him meant that he even wanted a relationship with her.

Against her better judgment, she found herself nodding. "All right."

He flashed a smile at her and took her by the hand. She set her beer bottle on a table as they passed by and then they were on the dance floor.

It was a lively two-step and they fell into the dance as if they'd been doing it together forever. She'd been country-western dancing since she was a little girl and it was obvious he was plenty experienced, too.

When the one dance was over, another tune started right away and he swung her into a country waltz. She found herself laughing as they danced and then she realized her headache had vanished. Every touch of his hands sent warmth throughout her body. Or was that just the heat of her skin from dancing?

She was ready to walk off the dance floor the moment the next song struck up, a slow tune, but Creed took her by the hand then brought her into his arms, catching her off guard. She braced her palms on his shoulders to keep him from holding her too close. He leaned down to whisper in her ear.

His warm breath caused a shiver to run through her as he murmured, "Thank you for the dances."

She swallowed, trying to not let his closeness affect her…the solidness of his body, his masculine scent, and the heat of his large hands at her waist. She cleared her throat but couldn't get anything out.

"I'd like to see you again," he said close to her ear.

She drew back and gave him a skeptical look. "You're a bull rider. You don't stay in one place for too long."

"Long enough," he said. "Where are you from?"

"I'm from southern Arizona, in the San Rafael Valley," she said. "But I now live in San Diego."

"There you go." He gave her a little grin. "We do have something in common. I'm from just north of Phoenix, in Kirkland, between Prescott and Wickenburg." He touched a lock of her long, dark hair. "What's an Arizona country girl doing in San Diego?"

"I work as a research associate at the University of California," she said. "In our department we do breeding maintenance, genotyping, cloning, and other related projects."

"I'm impressed." He continued to lightly play with her hair. "Did you go to the University of Arizona?"

She nodded. "Yes."

"I graduated from the U of A twelve years ago," he said with a grin. "I'd bet you were at least eight years behind me."

"Something like that." She smiled. "What was your major?"

"Animal Sciences."

The song ended, surprising her. The time had passed faster than she'd expected.

"I'd better go," she said as they drew apart.

"Why?" He walked beside her as she left the dance floor.

"It's getting late." And she was becoming far too interested in this bull rider.

He caught her by her hand and drew her to a stop. "Sure I can't talk you into a drink?"

"You already talked me into dancing with you." She smiled. "But no, not a drink."

"Give me your phone number," he said. "I want to see you again."

She shook her head. "I don't date bull riders."

With a laugh he said, "Why not?"

"It's too dangerous a sport," she said. "I'd be worried all the time."

"You'd worry about me?" He had that sexy grin again.

Somehow she felt off-balance by his reply. "I suppose I would, if we were dating. Which isn't a possibility because, like I said, I don't date bull riders."

"Why don't you give me a chance?" he said. "I'll show you that you don't have to worry about me."

She put her hands on her hips. "How many bones have you broken over the years? How many concussions have you had? How many times have you had to be stitched up?"

He winced.

"Or," she went on, "maybe you should just tell me what bones you *haven't* broken. Yet."

He shook his head. "It's not as bad as it sounds."

"Oh?" She folded her arms across her chest. "How many times have you ridden even when you were injured rather than waiting for those bones and injuries to heal?" She didn't wait for an answer. "More times than you can count, I'll bet."

He laughed and raised his hands. "Aw, come on, Danica. Just give me a chance."

She liked the way he said her name. His voice had a raw, sensual quality about it. "I'm heading up to my room now," she said. "It really was nice meeting you."

"So you're staying here," he said as she turned away and he fell into step beside her.

She realized her mistake when she'd said "up to my room." She paused mid-step and shook her head as she faced him. "Good night, Creed."

"I know when I'm not wanted." A smile was on his lips though when he said the words. "Good night, Danica."

As she walked out of the bar and made her way to the elevators, she found it hard not to look over her shoulder. She could feel him watching her and if she looked, she might find herself turning around and going back.

Excerpt... Satin and Saddles

Cheyenne McCray

Carly braced her hands on the back of Mike's chair as she watched the poker game with the Cameron men along a couple of their friends, including Mike. He was holding his own and it was down to him and Dillon who had the biggest pile of chips.

Throughout the game she'd had a hard time keeping her eyes off a Dillon and again he'd caught her at it. Like the other men, he'd taken off his western tux jacket leaving him in a shirt that was snug across his muscular chest and fit his broad shoulders just right. He had his shirtsleeves rolled up and she liked watching the way the muscles in his arms flexed when he dealt. Every now and then their gazes would meet and she'd feel a warm flush throughout her body.

She looked over Mike's shoulder. He had a straight flush. He set his cards down and shoved most of his chips into the middle of the table.

Dillon studied Mike for a moment, then his cards. "I'm all in," he said and pushed everything he had in.

Mike looked at the remainder of his chips then looked at Dillon.

"Have anything else you'd like to wager?" Dillon asked.

Mike glanced up at Carly then back to Dillon. "Got anything in mind?"

Dillon met Carly's gaze. "The rest of the weekend with Carly if I win. If you win you can buy Rocket."

Carly's jaw dropped and the other men around the table hooted and laughed.

"That is one deal too good to miss," Ty Sharpe, Mike's cousin, said. "Mike's been trying to buy that stallion off Dillon for the past year."

"I think *not*," she said.

"Come on, Carly." Wayne, Dillon's brother, grinned. "You'll sweeten the pot."

Zane nodded. "I'd like to see this."

Mike glanced up at Carly.

She put her hands on her hips. "Are you serious, Mike Sharpe? You'd trade me in a poker game?"

"Anything else you'd take?" Mike looked sheepish as he asked Dillon the question.

Dillon shook his head. "Carly or nothing."

Wayne laughed. "It's all in good fun, Carly."

She held back a smile. It was kind of funny—she'd never had men fight over her before—so to speak.

"Let me see your cards again, Mike." She sat on his knee and looked at his cards. A straight flush, ace to five. "All right." She glanced up at Dillon. "Do I have to sit in the middle of the table?"

The men chuckled.

"You're fine right where you are." Dillon leaned forward. "But when I win you have to come sit on *my* knee."

Carly felt her cheeks flush. She tilted her chin up. "Daytime only if you win. But when you lose, Mike gets to buy that horse."

"It's a deal." Dillon winked at her.

Mike laid down his cards. "Straight flush."

Dillon's eyes were totally on Carly as he laid down his own cards. "Royal flush."

Carly's eyes widened and this time she burned with heat all over. She had just been won in a poker game.

The men around the table were grinning and laughing. She tore her gaze from Dillon to Mike.

Mike wore a smile. "You know Dillon was just kidding."

Dillon shook his head. "I wasn't kidding."

She swallowed and met Dillon's blue eyes again. He patted his knee and beckoned to her.

"You can't be serious," Mike said. "That was a joke."

"Like I said, I wasn't kidding." Dillon looked at Carly. "You know I wasn't."

"You're right.." She stood. "When you made the bet I knew you were serious." She looked at Mike. "I guess I'm Dillon's for tomorrow."

"The deal was for the rest of the weekend," Dillon said.

Saturday and Sunday. She took a deep breath and walked over to him, hoping she wasn't blushing all over, and perched on his knee. He eased his arm around her waist and her whole body started tingling. Like earlier when she'd first talked to Dillon, she was at a loss for words at the moment, which was entirely unlike her.

She hadn't been this close to him before and she hadn't realized just how good he smelled. Of man and leather, a combination she loved.

Dillon stood, easing Carly to the floor and taking by the hand. "Time to cash out and head home." He looked at her. "How did you get here?"

"Mike." She glanced at Mike who had a bemused expression then she looked at Dillon. "He picked me up at my house."

Dillon slid his fingers over the back of her waist. "I'll get you home tonight and then in the morning, you're mine."

Excerpt... Champagne and Chaps

Cheyenne McCray

"That cowboy you just smiled at is on his way over." Carly's startling lavender eyes met Sabrina's gaze. "I knew you'd be flirting from the moment you walked in."

"I was not flirting." Sabrina's heart beat a little faster. "And you know I'm not ready to meet any guys."

Carly combed her fingers through her dark hair. "You're plenty ready. It's been seven months since you and the idiot broke up."

Idiot was right. Stephen was definitely one of those not-so-rare breeds.

Sabrina shook her head. "That's not all. You know what I mean."

"No, I don't know," Carly said. "There's no reason you can't get out and start living now."

Sabrina held one palm to her belly. "I don't know. I think it's too soon—"

"That is one incredibly fine cowboy," Carly interrupted. "Fine, fine, fine."

That was so true, Sabrina thought as she watched the man's easy approach from the corner of her eye.

He was tall and had a cowboy's build with broad shoulders and lean hips. He wore a white dress shirt and a white Stetson along with Wrangler jeans. The shirt in no way disguised his muscular chest and arms.

Yummy.

Sabrina's stomach flipped as the cowboy held her gaze and walked up to their table. He touched the brim of his hat as he looked from Sabrina to Carly.

"I'm Wyatt Cameron," he said with a sexy smile that made her stomach drop to her toes.

Carly extended her hand. "Carly Abbot."

Sabrina jumped when Carly elbowed her. Sabrina cleared her throat and offered her own hand. "Sabrina Holliday."

His touch was warm as he gripped her hand for a few moments and held her gaze. A shiver ran down her spine as she met his gorgeous brilliant blue eyes.

"Are you part of the Cameron crew that I hear so much about over in the San Rafael Valley?" Carly tilted her head to the side. "You have a bunch of brothers."

"That would be me." Wyatt had a spark of amusement in his eyes as he released Sabrina's hand. "Three brothers and a sister."

Carly smiled. "I figured."

"Mind if my friend and I sit with you?" Wyatt nodded in the direction of another good-looking cowboy who was leaning up against the bar.

"We don't mind at all," Carly said.

Sabrina felt mute. Wyatt Cameron had all the makings of a man she could really enjoy being around. But she didn't want that… Didn't want to get close to any man. She was all for Carly's determination that tonight was all about flirting and fun.

Wyatt took a seat at the high top and gave a signal to the other cowboy who started coming their way. When the cowboy arrived,

Wyatt made introductions.

"Mike, this is Sabrina and Carly." He gestured to each of them. "Sabrina and Carly, this is Mike Sharpe who's also from the valley."

"A pleasure." Mike smiled and shook each of their hands.

Carly gave a slow nod. "I think I've heard of your family, too," she said to Mike. "You own Sharpe Feed and Tack in Patagonia?"

"My cousin, Ty Sharpe, owns the feed store," Mike said. "I have a ranch on the other side of Wyatt's."

"The Sharpe family owns this bar, too, don't they?" Carly asked. "A friend mentioned it the last time I was here."

"That would be another cousin who owns Stampede." Mike glanced around the room. "Brady's probably around here somewhere."

"Where are you ladies from?" Wyatt's gaze settled on Sabrina.

Her cheeks warmed at the intense look of interest in his eyes. "Tucson."

"What part of town?" he asked.

She cleared her throat. "The foothills."

His gaze slid to Carly. "Whereabouts are you? Tucson, too?"

Carly shook her head. "Patagonia." She glanced at Sabrina. "Sabrina is staying with me for the summer."

Sabrina wanted to kick Carly under the table but she was afraid she would kick one of the men. She really didn't want these cowboys to know she'd be a lot closer to them than Tucson. This Wyatt might think she'd be interested in seeing him more, and all she wanted was a little fun.

But then again, she might be thinking too much into this. She'd barely met the guy. Still, she really didn't want to seem accessible to anyone. That was part of the reason why she'd let Carly talk her into staying for the summer. She needed time alone.

Wyatt's smile made Sabrina's toes curls. Damn, he was hot.

"Dance?" he asked and gestured to the floor as a new tune started.

Carly was busy chatting with Mike when Sabrina looked over at her friend.

I should just let loose just like we planned, Sabrina thought. She missed her old self. There was a time when she would have been flirting like Carly and just having fun without worrying about the possibility that the guy would want to get into a relationship. She needed that again. She needed to let her hair down and just have fun.

With a smile she looked back at Wyatt. "Sure."

He surprised her by helping her down from the tall stool at the high top, then took her hand and led her to the dance floor.

Butterflies batted around in Sabrina's belly as they made it onto the floor, and he brought her close and they started to two-step. "I'm not very good at this." She raised her voice over the loud music as she stepped on Wyatt's boot. "To me two-stepping means one step on the floor and one on your boot."

"You're doing fine." He met her gaze, a glint of humor in his eyes. "Just don't run off is all I ask. I'd like to get to know you."

She didn't answer. She didn't plan on letting any man get to know her well. But it wouldn't hurt to have a little fun dancing with a cowboy. This was all about a fun night out.

"I'll think about it," she said with an answering smile.

By the time three songs had passed, Sabrina was laughing and enjoying herself more than she'd expected. Her skin was covered in a light film of perspiration and her heart was beating a little faster from the fast-paced tunes that they'd danced to.

She'd been having so much fun that she forgotten all about Carly. When she glanced back at the table, her friend was gone. She searched the dance floor with her gaze and smiled when she saw her friend talking with Mike to one side of the room.

Carly looked like she was having fun flirting with the cowboy, which was no surprise. If Carly was anything when it came to men, she was a flirt and a heartbreaker. Poor Mike, Sabrina thought and mentally shook her head. You're in for some heartache if you're not careful. Unless Carly actually considered settling for one man.

Ha. That'll be the day. Not after Carly's breakup. Ever since then she'd decided to flirt and play and that was good enough for her.

Sabrina caught her breath as Wyatt brought her into his embrace, catching her off guard. For a moment she wondered what he was doing and then realized the band had struck up a slow tune.

He drew her close and she felt his belt buckle dig into her belly and smelled the clean scent of his aftershave. Her stomach flip-flopped again as she felt a moment of panic. This was close, far too close to be allowing herself to get to a man.

But it felt so good being in his arms. She rested her palms on his shoulders and could feel the power in his body as they slowly moved on the dance floor. About six-three, he was almost a foot taller than she was and she felt more than petite in his arms. She breathed in his warm, masculine scent as they danced and found herself sighing. She loved the scent of a man.

ABOUT CHEYENNE

New York Times and *USA Today* bestselling author Cheyenne McCray's books have received multiple awards and nominations, including

*RT Book Reviews magazine's Reviewer's Choice awards for Best Erotic Romance of the year and Best Paranormal Action Adventure of the year

*Three "RT Book Reviews" nominations, including Best Erotic Romance, Best Romantic Suspense, and Best Paranormal Action Adventure.

*Golden Quill award for Best Erotic Romance

*The Road to Romance's Reviewer's Choice Award

*Gold Star Award from Just Erotic Romance Reviews

*CAPA award from The Romance Studio

Cheyenne grew up on a ranch in southeastern Arizona. She has been writing ever since she can remember, back to her kindergarten days when she penned her first poem. She always knew one day she would write novels, hoping her readers would get lost in the worlds she created, just as she experienced when she read some of her favorite books.

Chey has three sons, two dogs, and is an Arizona native who loves the desert, the sunshine, and the beautiful sunsets. Visit Chey's website and get all of the latest info at CheyenneMcCray. com and meet up with her at Cheyenne McCray's Place on Facebook! Feel free to contact Chey at chey@cheyennemccray.com

CPSIA information can be obtained at www.ICGtesting.com
Printed in the USA
LVOW08s1013171113

361642LV00001B/237/P